CHOSEN MAGIC

DEMON BAYOU SERIES BOOK THREE

S LAWRENCE

For information contact :

sglawrenceauthor@gmail.com

https://www.slawrencewriter.com/ sign up for my newsletter to stay up to date on new releases and for exclusive giveaways

Cover design by Sanja Balan (Sanja's Covers)

ISBN:978-1-950851-03-4

First Edition: 2019

❀ Created with Vellum

*H*e should have woken by now.

His injuries were severe but have healed, so I'm afraid he has given up. He is choosing to stay in that place between worlds. He has grown tired over the years, hiding his growing despondence from those around him, retreating from them and everything else more and more.

Even without his memories, he was drawn to those he was given to protect. It was in a tiny village that I first saw him and followed him to the others.

I had been living with the First People for hundreds of years by then, moving from tribe to tribe whenever I felt power linger near me for too long.

I didn't run from him though; something about the way he played with the children touched me.

He has always helped when he could, but the destruction of the people, of the tribes, hurts him. Each one he couldn't save destroyed a small piece of him.

Now he understands why. They were his to save, and he failed them.

At least, that's what he thinks. I smile as she comes in, carrying a bowl of cold spring water and a rag to wash his face.

It is almost time.

CHAPTER 1

CHARLIE

*S*taring in the mirror, I don't know why I'm even bothering, but it doesn't stop me. Dagen bought all this stuff. I glance at the clothes hanging behind me and smile. He asked me if I was adventurous once; tonight he's testing to see how far I'm willing to go.

I focus on my face, working on the "beard" I'm creating. If he wants a man tonight, I'll give him just that. I think I would do anything for him.

Rio is a city of sin, and he is a demon.

I smile as I transform.

He is waiting in the living room when I finally emerge. We've rented a house, and so did Lillian and Torryn. I think Torryn is upset we didn't want to share, but I don't care and neither does Dagen. He is sprawled on a low couch, legs spread wide and head dropped back on a cushion, eyes closed.

He hears me coming, I know that for certain, but he doesn't react; he just waits.

"So where are we going?" I ask, keeping my voice a couple octaves lower than my normal speaking voice.

A slow smile spreads over his face, and my heart pounds. I was right—I would do anything for that. His eyes open and the scent of chocolate hits me hard. Oh, he likes this very much.

His eyes travel over the clothes he picked out—tailored slacks, dress shirt, and vest. I don't miss the pause at my crotch and fight not to grin. He wasn't expecting me to be packing apparently. Well, this girl doesn't do anything half-assed.

"I found a club." Do tell.

"Oh, yeah? What kind?" The look he gives me is positively wicked, and I shiver. "Oh." I lose my deeper voice in my excitement, and he raises a brow. I shrug because he can't blame me. "I'm ready when you are." Sin is here and ready to play.

He crooks a finger, and I walk to him, climb over his legs, and seat myself snug against him.

"I almost don't want to take you out now." His breath whispers over my neck as he nips at the sensitive flesh there.

I roll my hips a little, pushing the prosthetic against him, and he groans. "I got all ready, so take me out and show me off." He growls just before biting me hard enough to mark me as his. I smile as I climb off and hold out my hand. His slips into it, squeezing it tightly for a moment.

I realize in that instant he had been very worried about my reaction. I've never considered myself to be gay or straight, bi or anything else. I just am. I find people beautiful and I tend to be drawn to their souls more than their bodies. I love who I love. Period. I'm attracted to who attracts me, male, female, human or demon. I chuckle at the thought, and he glances at me as we walk out to the car. I just shake my head.

I stare at the car when we stop. It is low-slung and sleek, fast and powerful, just like the man at my side. I have no idea where he found it in such a short time. But I love the way the leather hugs me as I slide into the seat.

He closes the door after watching my reaction. I don't miss his as he adjusts it when he gets in a few seconds later.

The rumble of the engine vibrates through me, and I hold on as we race down the hill. Curving through switchbacks, he is driving like what he is. Demon.

I fucking love it.

The club is not what I was expecting. We pull into an underground garage, and he parks and helps me out. When we reach an elevator, he reaches in his breast pocket, pulls out a card, and scans it.

This is some Fifty Shades shit, is all I can think as we step in and the elevator starts without us doing anything. There are no numbers, no buttons, and he leans back, just watching me.

I mirror his stance, only jumping slightly when the thing dings and stops. The jump totally blows my attempt at nonchalance. I don't care. I'm nervous, but it's excitement that's driving it. He pushes off the wall and steps up to me.

"Last chance. We can leave." I shake my head. "It's fine if you don't want to do this."

I know it would be. "Dagen, I'm not even sure what this is but I'm not scared or freaked out. I want to do whatever this is with you." His face lights up, and I once again know I'd do anything.

The doors slide open, and I feel my mouth drop open. Holy shit. Okay, this is more than Fifty Shades. I don't even know where to look.

It certainly shouldn't have been at the couple in the furry suits.

CHAPTER 2

MEDICINE WOMAN

I keep waiting for my punishment. Death lurks in every shadow, although the Creator has never been one to hide...exactly.

I know when it comes, it will be...well...biblical.

I smile as I hear giggling coming from somewhere far outside this temple. Few venture inside this sacred place now.

I came here so many years ago; I can remember when it was full of members of all the surrounding tribes. People would come from great distances to see the priestess that had the power to heal.

Glancing at the altar, which is now holding the stubborn demon, my face softens as I watch Citlali wipe at his brow.

She is the last of her very long line, one that started with Raphael. Crossing, I touch her shoulder, drawing her attention.

"I'm going to be gone for a day or so. I need to check on his people." She looks back at the man that has been under her care for days now.

"Who are his people?" It is the first question she's asked about her charge.

"They are very important. Not just to me but to us all." I reach out and brush the tendrils of hair that have come loose from his braids away from his eyes. "He is special."

"Special to who?" She studies him closer. I shrug and she rolls her eyes. "Fine. Keep your secrets; you always do."

"He should be awake by now." I say what I've been thinking.

"You should've taken him to the hospital."

"Why? I have the best doctor right here." She shakes her head.

"Citlali, you come from a line of healers that started at the beginning of time." She raises her brow. "Just watch over him, please."

She nods, once again focusing on her patient. I step back on silent feet until I can fade away without her noticing.

I stop first in the city just down the mountain. Two houses filled with love shine like beacons in the night. The prophecy is beginning to be fulfilled. Those babies I hid so long ago and kept safe until the destined ones were born are finding their way to those that can take over their protection.

Farther north I travel in the blink of an eye, stopping in New Orleans to check on Evander. His broken heart calls to more than me. I don't fail to notice the angel that lingers near. Caliel is unaware of myself and the one that watches him. She hides her form but not the love that shines from her. I shake my head at the oblivion the men seem to be lost in. Evander is wrapped in heartache and anger; I understand both. He has been robbed twice now. I wish I could have stopped it but I had been hiding from my brother and the Fallen.

My brother. Those words hurt.

It took me a long time to admit that he was unsaveable, even longer to separate my love for him from what I know must happen.

What I must do. What I will do.

I hope I'm strong enough.

Shaking my head, I refocus on Evander, wishing there was something I could do for him. I've liked him since the beginning, since I saw how much he cared for the others. He worked so hard to keep them safe, not just from dangers but from their pasts.

He made them the men they are, to an extent.

I let myself drift away. I've stayed away as long as I can. He makes me nervous. He knows too much.

The desert is quiet and breathtaking in the evening, the sky a mixture of pinks and oranges. I stand at the edge of the cliff, looking out at the beautiful creation of the Father. I hate that tears fill my eyes at the thought of Him. I hate that I still miss being in His presence.

Movement forces me to turn, and there he is. The Morning Star. God's favorite. The one that was strong enough to stand up for what was right. My eyes widen as I watch him sway from side to side, a baby held snugly in his arms.

The look on his face is absolutely angelic. Then the sound of his voice reaches me, and my breath catches in my throat. It is so amazing that I don't realize I'm moving until my feet hit the concrete that surrounds the pool. Freezing, I listen to my heart pound as he looks up.

His eyes lock on the area where I stand, invisible to everyone, watching him like I've done for so long. His brow furrows and his eyes narrow as he studies the area. The baby makes a noise, upset that he has stopped singing.

"Shh, Chana, it's alright, baby girl." His voice rumbles as

he responds, never taking his eyes off me. Or at least where I would be, if he could see me. "You are playing with fire."

I smile when those almost silver wings flare out, lifting him and the child into the air. I choose to ignore the warning.

"Goodbye, Morning Star."

CHAPTER 3

ARKYN

I don't want to live.

I'm ready to greet the darkness. I have failed at every task set before me, either by God or by Lucifer.

I'm not worthy of this world, much less some destined mate. I would only fail them too.

The light fades until only grayness, a single shade lighter than black, surrounds me. I welcome it, pulling it around me like a shroud.

Just letting myself drift away.

Selfish asshole that I am, I hardly feel any remorse for leaving…well…the entire world in the lurch. What I do feel is like an icepick straight through my heart.

But, in typical Arkyn fashion, I will let them all down. I always do.

I wonder if God gave me the job He did because He knew I would fail. Maybe He needed someone to fail them. Probably was His plan all along.

'*I'm sorry, brothers.*'

I pray, the word sticks in my throat, they can forgive me.

I can actually feel my tethers breaking as I give in to the desire I've had for as long as I can remember.

'Arkyn, why won't you come back to us?'

Who the fuck is she? I don't recognize the voice and I have no idea how she is speaking directly to me or how she knows my fucking name.

I let my mind roam the darkness and then there I see a tiny flame, so hot and bright that it is white. What the hell?

'Your friends must miss you. Sitara says you are very important.'

Who the fuck is Sitara?

'She wouldn't have brought you here and saved you if you weren't, so it's time for you to come back to us. To her.'

I'm so far from important. No one needs me to come back. The flame flickers, and I'm suddenly scared it will die out. I try to ignore that fear, to ignore the light.

Stay away from the light, Carol Anne, and all that.

'Sorry, I can't come back and I'm so far from important. To anyone.'

I just barely whisper the thought out at her.

The light winks out, and I'm so disappointed. What a fucking girl I am.

'Arkyn?' The voice is filled with both terror and excitement, and suddenly the darkness is blasted away and the heat of her flame warms me. *'How? What? I don't understand.'*

Neither do I. Shit. I guess I ain't dying today.

CHAPTER 4

CITLALI

I drop the cloth and run. My fear far outweighs any curiosity my mind might have.

I run until I'm to my truck parked a few miles from the hidden temple. I ignored all the looks from the people that had been outside the temple leaving offerings to the healer, to Sitara.

My hand shakes as I fumble in my shorts, trying to dig the keys out. I gasp for air and I know rationally I'm having a panic attack, to go along with the fact I'm not used to running anywhere that far.

Her cryptic words woven into everyday conversation for my entire life play out in my head. It's a head that has been shaking from side to side since I heard his voice.

Her last words stand out—since the beginning of time. Nope. No. No way. She has told me the story of the beginning of time many times since I was a child, of how before the ancestors there had been others but the gods had grown angry at them. How they had built the temple, how it had been entrusted to her people. Right, her people. I have explored areas that even she doesn't go to. She should because if she did, she'd have known about the paintings. Crude at first, but then more and more detailed.

Paintings of her, not her people. Long ago, I realized she does not age. She makes it look as if she does but she doesn't. Maybe she's not good at it because she didn't used to have to worry about it, as my people died young.

But, like she said, I'm a very good doctor and I've studied her since I was a child after my mother brought me to Sitara.

I, the last of my family, was given to the healer to keep safe. I've often wondered if my mother knew who she gave me to, what she gave me to.

I've had a wonderful life with Sitara and the people she had raise me but I've known for some time she has bigger plans for me. She shaped and molded me into the person I am.

I have a very bad feeling that the man laying on the stone table is a huge part of that plan.

'Where are you going?' Oh shit, the key shakes as I try to get it into the ignition.

"Where are your steady surgeon hands, Citlali?" I grumble as I try to stop the shaking.

Finally, success, the key slips in and I turn it. Stomping the gas, I back up and spin the wheel. My head almost hits the glass of the window, and I slam on the brakes. Calm the fuck down, girl. Jesus, you're going to kill yourself.

And there, stuck under that thought, is my fear. Not that I am but that he is meant to. What if I am a sacrifice?

It seems ludicrous, and yet my people made human sacrifices long after the world believes we stopped. Would Sitara do that to me?

I don't even want to think it but... I'm not taking the chance. The tires throw mud and gravel as I push the pedal almost to the floor and race away. Everything in me is screaming… HIDE!

I drive like I'm possessed to my home. Parking in the garage, I stumble out of the truck in my haste. She knows where I live. All rational thought has fled my mind. All I know is I must get away from her and him.

Punching the code on the alarm, I unlock the door and step inside. Closing it, I fall against the cool steel. The adrenaline starts to crash, and I begin to cry, emotion flooding my brain.

She is my only family. How could she betray me like this, leaving me to him?

As the first tear falls onto the tile of the floor, I push away from the door, determined and heartbroken as I make my way through my home to the bedroom. Grabbing a bag, I begin to throw things in it. I don't pay attention to what, just grabbing things that I can barely see through the tears.

Freezing, I close my eyes and focus. Sitara has an energy I noticed years ago. I got very good at knowing when she had come to visit.

I haven't been fast enough. Whirling, I decide to face her, to demand answers as to why.

Too late, I realize my mistake.

"Who are you?" He smiles, and I've never seen anything so purely evil.

"My name isn't important to someone like you." The look he gives me tells me he thinks even less than that of me. "What you should ask is what am I?"

I don't give him the satisfaction. He waits, watching as I stand in silence, my brain going a million miles an hour as I try to figure out a way to get away from him. I feel physically sick just being in the room with him. How could I have ever mistaken his energy for Sitara?

He crosses to the window that looks out at the mountain where I had left Arkyn and the safety of the temple. I run. I don't look back. I'm out the door in seconds, making my way past my truck, never slowing until he appears right in front of me.

A blood curdling scream tears from my throat as I stop. The force of my body plus the abrupt stop has me falling forward. He just watches as I crash into the dirt and rocks, a grin blooming across his face as I try to scramble away the instant after impact.

I can taste blood in my mouth, and my hands are leaving dark imprints on the dry ground.

He stalks me. There is no other way to describe his almost slow-motion steps as he comes at me. I draw a breath as the scream dies away.

"You going somewhere, human?" Human. All my suspicions are confirmed with one word.

"Get away from me. Sitara…" His laughter makes my skin crawl.

"Sitara will do nothing. I knew she kept a pet but I couldn't find you or her, until today. Thank you for that."

I'm shaking my head in denial. No way I did something to alert him to my location.

"You spoke to one of those filthy demons." He answers my unspoken question.

Arkyn. The man before me nods as he sees me figure out who he's talking about.

"Which one was it?" So you don't know everything, asshole. The seconds tick by, and I watch as he begins to get angry. He's on me in the blink of my eye. Literally.

Open, he's a few feet in front of me. Blink, and he is squatting right over me. His hands whip out, grabbing my arms just as I try to force my body back.

15

"You will tell me…" He spits as he speaks, his face inches from mine. "Eventually."

Just as I feel my very cells seemingly break apart, I send him a message.

'Tell Sitara I'm sorry. I should have trusted her.'

CHAPTER 5

ARKYN

I hear her again, the absolute terror and regret clearing the darkness surrounding me.

I start to swim towards the surface, towards consciousness. A feeling of urgency has my adrenaline rushing through my body.

It takes an enormous amount of effort to pry my eyes open, and when I do, I see the woman materialize at my side. The woman that had taken Charlie from the parking garage.

The one who has watched us.

A new emotion joins the fear for the one who has been connecting with me. Anger.

Her eyes connect with mine and she starts to gasp, but it's cut off when my hand locks around her throat.

"Who are you?" I demand while my eyes bounce around the area. "Where the hell am I?"

It's my turn to be surprised when I feel her power surge and my hand is forced from her skin.

Delicate fingers brush over the skin reddened from my grasp.

"I'm the one who saved you. Who saved Charlie. I'm trying to help you all." An answer without an answer.

Pushing up, I keep my eyes on her. "What are you? You are no angel and you certainly aren't a demon."

She sighs as I swing my legs over the side of the stone altar I've been lying on.

"Listen, lady, answer or not. I need to go. Someone has been connecting with me and she's in trouble."

Her eyes widen and then close, and I watch as she becomes extremely upset. Her eyes open and the fear there makes me dial my anger back some.

"Did you heal me?" She nods but is distracted, and I feel her power expand. I know she searches for the other woman. "Is she like you?"

This time her head shakes from side to side. "Are you Sitara?"

When her eyes lock onto me, I see my first glimpse of the real being standing before me.

I'm almost mesmerized by the swirling opal colors of those eyes. I know her entire appearance is a mask of her power, hiding her true form. Those eyes though, they hold the truth.

"Where did you hear that name?" Her voice carries power, and I can tell if I didn't answer her willingly, she could rip the information from me with almost zero effort.

"The last thing I heard was *'Tell Sitara I'm sorry. I should have trusted her.'*" I watch her crumble.

"Yes, I'm Sitara. I left her with you, hoping she could draw you back." She looks at me, and I see knowledge. She had known what I had chosen. "I hid the first of her line and have protected them all along. I chose to live among the First People, loving their beliefs and way of life. I came south as they did. I healed when I could. Her people built this temple for the healer. For me. I was the healer for many tribes. It was where I first saw you."

I stare at her. "When?"

"Long before this world was discovered." She has watched me for hundreds of years without me knowing.

That's my first thought, and then shame overwhelms me. She has seen my failures.

"You didn't know your task, so how could it be considered a failure?"

I refuse to answer. "Who is the woman? How do I find her?"

"Citlali. I have raised her since she was a baby. She is the last descendant of Raphael." I feel my mouth fall open. "And as I had hoped, if she connected with you, she is your Chosen."

I blink and I feel like it is in slow motion.

"Mine." I stumble over the word, but my demon almost purrs in satisfaction.

He has been silent for a very long time, resigned with failure like I am. We both get very angry as we realize she has been stolen from us.

"The Fallen?" I look at her and I can see the red of my eyes reflected in her pastel ones.

Her head shakes. "No. They alone couldn't hide her from me." She pauses, swallowing as her eyes begin to fill with tears.

The woman is dead. I'm ready to dive back into the darkness.

"I'm afraid only one could hide her from me." Not dead, I realize as a rush of relief pulls me from the edge. "My brother."

Her demeanor and the fear in her voice steal some of my happiness at hearing the woman is alive.

I refuse to fail her.

CHAPTER 6

DAGEN

*I*t's too much. I'm going to lose her now.

I pause just across the threshold as she stares at some couple dressed as, I think maybe foxes, doing I'm not sure exactly. Her mouth is hanging open, and I can see the shock stamped across her face.

"We can go," I murmur, grabbing her arm and pulling.

"What? No way are we leaving." She spins looking up at my face, Sin is in full effect. "We are so checking all of this out. And you are showing me whatever it was that you wanted to see or…" She pulls her lower lip between her perfectly imperfect teeth as she pauses, and my heart is pounding. "Do. We are going to have so much fun tonight."

I don't know what to say. She grins as she grabs my face and drags me down for a kiss that is filled with every dark thought I've ever had. That kiss, that devouring of my fears, frees something in me. Then she breaks away, spinning to face the room once more.

"Mr. Winter, we have your table just this way." I glance to my left at the man that has materialized there while we were distracted. "If you'll follow me." He starts away, not looking to see if we obeyed his request.

He leads us through the main part of the club. We pass people covered with silken ropes, some hanging from the ceiling, a man strapped to a Saint Andrew's Cross, blindfolded and gagged. Behind sheer curtains that hide nothing are multiple couples fucking. One woman catches my eye and winks as her partner pounds into her from behind. Male and male, female and female, every way, any way is represented.

Charlie's eyes bounce around the room, trying to take it all in, even after we slide into our semi-private area. A low velvet couch with a high tufted back curves around a glass table. Drinks appear almost immediately, and she reaches blindly for a glass, not willing to miss a thing. Taking her hand, I direct it to the mint julep waiting for her. She never looks, just brings the glass to her lips, sipping.

The moment the liquid hits her tongue, her eyes turn to mine, and what I see in them takes my breath for a moment. Love. Unconditional.

"So, what are we looking for?" She whispers, smiling over the edge of the glass, her eyebrow raised.

"Anything that you want," I answer noncommittally.

"No. Tonight isn't about me. It's about you, so what do you want?" She sets her glass down and scoots against my side, leaning her head against my shoulder. We present an interesting picture, I'm sure.

Her eyes travel over the room as she waits for me to answer. I notice when she pauses briefly on a beautiful couple. The man is kissing the woman's neck, but both are looking at us.

"Do you want them?" She murmurs, still watching them. "They want us."

I agree with her assessment. "Are you sure? We can just

watch, no need to join any others." I give her an out, not wanting to lose her to my darker desires.

"Dagen, I wouldn't be here if I wasn't willing."

"And if I want him?" I hold my breath, waiting for her answer.

"Then take him. I'm sure she won't mind." She smiles at the woman as she raises her hand. I watch frozen as Charlie, my perfect other half, beckons them over.

The man straightens, a satisfied gleam in his eyes. The woman starts our way, hips rolling, the scent of lust rolling off her like a storm.

The man's dark eyes lock on me, and I see interest.

Charlie holds out her hand. She does not choose one, instead waits to see which will come to her. I do nothing, making it perfectly clear who is in charge of what happens tonight.

I'm surprised when the man crosses in front of his partner. Taking the hand that is outstretched, he pulls Charlie away from me. My muscles tighten for a moment.

I relax only when he slides onto the couch and pulls her to him. I watch, growing hard as he kisses her all the while keeping his eyes locked on mine. His partner climbs onto my recently freed lap and hums when she feels my hardness press into her core.

Seconds tick by, turning to minutes, as hands roam over heated flesh. I bury my fingers into the woman's hair and pull her head back hard, testing her limits. She pants in response, and I smile at her partner as I sink my teeth into the flesh of her shoulder.

Her cry draws Charlie's eyes, eyes that are clouded with need. Her hand is working over the man's dick through his pants.

"Dagen." I only need to hear that and I raise my hand. An attendant appears instantly.

"A room, please," I murmur as I release the woman's neck. She will carry the mark for a while.

We all rise as the attendant nods and turns to lead us to a more private venue. We barely make it through the doors before we come together a mass of desire and sin.

None of us are interested in wasting time. Clothes are removed, and the man's face turns almost feral at the sight of Charlie stripped before him.

I am suddenly not sure of my willingness to share. She senses my mood immediately and turns to me and the woman, taking our hands and drawing us both to the bed. At the edge, she turns to us both, and I just watch to see what my woman is about to do. She smiles at the man waiting behind us, blowing him a cheeky kiss as she lays back.

She keeps at the edge of the mattress, while drawing the woman with her. I understand and I feel myself harden even more as I stroke over my dick.

The woman takes her place, turning to face me while positioning her core over Charlie's face. It's my turn to glance back at the man, and if I thought he looked feral before, now he looks savage as he stalks toward me.

"Dagen." It's a moan as Charlie reaches up, gripping the woman's hips and drawing her core down to her mouth. Her tongue flicks out, and as I watch her draw it through the woman's soaked folds, I position myself at Charlie's equally wet channel. I slam inside my woman, watching as she slips two fingers in the woman and fucks her in rhythm with me. The woman lets her eyes fall closed as I reach out and roll her hardened nipple between my finger and thumb. I mirror the action on Charlie's and hear her moan against the woman's mound.

I feel him draw near, then feel his heat at my back. I have a moment of apprehension, but then he is pushing me forward. The woman takes my mouth as he lines up at my opening. His hand reaches around and he slides his fingers through Charlie's lips, gathering moisture on them. I feel the moisture coat me just before he pushes in.

I lose my rhythm as he pushes further until he is fully seated, and then we all begin to move. Moans and grunts fill the air along with the sounds of flesh slapping against flesh.

I'm not going to last. It has been too long, and I feel Charlie's body tightening around me. The woman begins to keen and her body stiffens. She shakes as Charlie continues her assault until finally she falls to the side. Turning as she does, she locks her mouth on my woman's, kissing her deeply, while her fingers play over Charlie's small breasts. I brace myself on my arms over them as he pounds into me. Each time, the force of it pushes me deeper into Charlie's swollen, velvet channel.

As she tightens even more around me, I feel my orgasm begin to build and I reach back, jerking him even harder into me.

He fills me as I fill her, and she explodes, screaming...my name.

CHAPTER 7

CITLALI

I wish he would kill me for real.

How long has it been? Hours? Days? Weeks? Maybe months? I don't know.

I know the things I feel aren't real. He has me trapped in some place where time doesn't exist. I've died hundreds of times in nightmarish ways. Each time, I wake up and another horrifying day of fighting for my life begins.

They all end the same—me dead.

I just woke and glancing around, I see this time I'm on the beach. I've learned not to venture into the water. I try for the countless time to reach Sitara or Arkyn.

Nothing.

I've reached my breaking point and I hate him for it. Hopefully, it has been years to get here. I'd hate myself more if it only took him hours to turn me into this.

I will not fight the death, instead I'm going to enjoy the sun while I have it. Not every rendition of the day has sunlight or the sound of waves crashing against the shore.

I let my eyes close, refusing to watch for the death I know

is coming. I quit playing his sickening game and let the fake sun warm me.

I didn't see it.

I awake to ice and snow. I didn't fight it when it arrived.

I awake choking on water and let it pull me under.

I wake tied to a bed. I feel my old resistance try to struggle to life but I shove it down. I will give him no satisfaction.

'Arkyn? Can you hear me?' I call out, keeping my eyes closed even when I hear footsteps approaching. *'I wish, well, I wish we could have actually met. That I could have brought you back. I like to think you could have stopped him.'*

I find myself talking to him day after day. Telling him stories from my life. If he had been able to hear me, he would know just about everything by now.

I picture him, making his eyes dark even though I've never seen them. In my mind, he's smiling, his hand held out just waiting for me to take it, offering me salvation from my hell. Even though I know it is a delusion, I still reach for that life line.

For just one instant, I feel the warmth of his skin. *'Citlali?'*

I jerked my head at the sound of his worry-filled voice. *'Arkyn?'*

I wait and wait for an answer, but it never comes. Maybe I imagined the first one. The door begins to open, and I turn my head as my heart begins to pound. Arkyn stands there, outlined by light.

"Are you really here?" He smiles and steps in, closing the door behind him.

Relief rushes through me until his face shifts to something I don't or can't recognize. Pulling at the ropes, I begin to struggle even as I begin to understand.

This is just a new version of my hell. Forcing my muscles to relax, I stop struggling.

"Why don't you just tell me your name?"

He finally shows me his true face as he draws near. "Theon." He bows his head slightly.

"Sitara is your sister?" He nods, and a wicked smile splits his face.

"Oh, yes, and I've searched for her and the ones she hid from me for a very long time." His fingertips skate over my ankle, and I fight the shiver of revulsion.

The ones. More than one. More than me. "There are others?"

My goal is to keep him talking, but if I learn more about all this, it will be a bonus.

"Did my dear little sister never tell you the story of our people?" I shake my head. "It's tragic and yet as old as time. A jealous father who punishes his children because they dared to reach higher than him."

His face twists in anger as his fingers tighten painfully on my leg, and I'm worried that this story might end badly for me.

"Sitara chose the wrong side in this war." He glares at me.

I am the wrong side.

"It would be easier to show you." I'm instantly in a beautiful city. Just looking at it, I know it isn't one I would find anywhere in the world.

He still has a tight grip, but it's now on my shoulders as he crowds me from behind. Pressing his body against mine from top to bottom, his hot breath puffs against my ear as he begins to talk about where we are.

"This was our home, a bright and shining example of what we were capable of." Two children run down the street in front of us, hand in hand, and his fingers dig in for a second before loosening slightly.

"That is Sitara and me." I watch the children play with

new interest. "Of course, this was long before she betrayed me."

The scene changes, and the city is in ruins, completely destroyed. People lay dead in the streets, and now he begins to almost growl.

"What happened?" I whisper.

"God." The word is spit out. I can't stop myself from turning to look at his face.

"God? The God?" He nods, the vein along his temple pulsing with rage.

"We were His first children." His hands slide away. Glancing up at his face, I see that he's focused on the scene and I'm almost forgotten. "Sitara and I had gone to visit the others. It's the only reason we survived. They hid us for years. Then the angels came. Gave us the chance to avenge our entire race, and Sitara turned her back on them. On me."

"I'm so sorry." His head turns and he looks at me like he had forgotten me. "I didn't know."

"I'm not surprised she didn't tell you of her betrayal."

"Who were the ones that hid you? Where was that place?" He frowns.

"It doesn't matter who they were, for they are gone. The place was what you humans called Avalon."

"Like with King Arthur?" I can't hide my surprise.

He actually rolls his eyes. "That was a story, but I suppose if that's what you need to understand what I'm talking about, then fine."

"Excuse me for trying to understand why you are doing this," I grumble and regret it immediately.

His hand is around my throat before the last syllable is out of my throat.

"I don't care if you understand." Spit coats my face, and I struggle to break his grip. "You are nothing. A means to an end. Bait."

Darkness winks across my vision, and I know he has his fingers perfectly placed over my carotid arteries.

Swinging my fist with all my might, I punch him straight in his nose, and a smile curves my lips. The blood that floods out is my last sight before my brain and body shut down.

Maybe this time will be my last death.

CHAPTER 8

ARKYN

I had her for one second after all this time. I had her.

My fist pounds into the stone wall and the rock crumbles. Another failure.

I continue to hit the ancient stones until Luc's power wraps around me, holding me frozen. Even the blood that had been dripping on the stone floor freezes.

"Arkyn, you must calm down before you destroy this place. I'm assuming Sitara wouldn't like that." He looks around, but of course, she is nowhere in sight. She leaves each time he has come.

Slowly, his power eases, and I flex my already-swelling hands. Bone rubs against bone, but I ignore the pain.

'He's right; I wouldn't.'

'Get here then and help me. Help her.' I've grown tired of her cat and mouse games with the King of Hell. *'Stop hiding from him.'*

She grows quiet, and I worry that I might have pushed her too far this time. I've made comments as the days turned to weeks, but this is the first time I've been completely direct.

Her power wraps around me. Holding my hands up, I watch in fascination as the bones knit and the skin grows together. She appears right in front of me, and I jerk in surprise.

Her hands are a hair's breadth from mine as she finishes the healing. Glancing back over my shoulder, I almost laugh at the expression on Luc's face.

"Luc, meet Sitara." She glances up at him, and he just stares, dumbfounded.

Finally, he speaks, only to say, "I remember you."

She shakes her head. "I'm sorry, but we've never met."

His head shakes. "No, I'm sorry, I meant I remember your people." He steps closer, and I can feel her tense. Looking at her, I try to judge if she is afraid or if it's just him. I see fear and before I can even recognize what I'm doing, I step between them.

"I wouldn't hurt her." He is both outraged and hurt, and I hate that it is my fault.

Opening my mouth, I start to speak, but he disappears and I'm left looking at empty space.

"Why did you do that?" Confusion is woven into the question, and when I look at her, I see it clouds her eyes.

"You were scared." My tone has a bit more bite than I intend.

"I'm not scared of him. Exactly." I raise a brow and wait for the rest of her explanation. She draws a deep breath before sighing loudly. "God sent His angels to destroy us. Or so we thought. My brother and I weren't there that day. Now I'm not so sure." She paces away.

Spinning, she faces me, and I can tell she's ready to spill her guts but I hold up my hand. She needs to know about Citlali.

"I connected with her for just an instant." Her eyes widen.

31

"She's alive, but I'm not sure for how much longer. We have to find her now."

"I've been thinking. He's hiding her, but unlike how I hid by suppressing most of my power, I think he is drawing from the Fallen." My fingers run up and down over my braids.

Fuck, that's not good news. My hand stops, and I look down. A new bead is attached to the left one. Lifting it up, I bring it close to my face and study it. It is a bright green stone and on it, a drum is carved.

"Did you do this?" She shakes her head as she comes closer, and a smile slowly spreads across her face. It makes her look even younger than she already does. She is a lot like Luc in that aspect.

"It was Citlali. When she was in school, she studied all the tribes of the Americas. They were all her people, she said."

The drum is used to talk with the Great Spirit. A prayer, in a way. I swallow hard at the emotion rolling through me.

"She would have asked Him to heal you, bring you back." My fingers close on the stone tightly.

"Lot of good it did her," I growl.

"You're here, aren't you?" Is she serious?

"You're kidding, right? We both know you healed me. He did nothing. Just like always." She shrugs, and it pisses me off more. "For fuck's sake, Sitara, He killed your entire race except for you and your demented brother. Kicked Luc right out of Heaven and into Hell for questioning Him and then left the whole world to the Fallen." The last word is screamed and it echoes off the stone walls.

Her hair stands on end as my power slips my control. Sparks light up the darkness of the temple.

"Arkyn, please." From someone else, it would sound rude but from her, it is a quiet plea for me not to destroy more of her temple.

Deep breaths. Count to ten. My brothers would never let me live it down if they could hear those words.

"Sorry." I don't say it until her long hair is once again lying against her back.

"Let's skip anything to do with the Father. What I had started to tell you about the Fallen and my brother," I feel like a child being scolded even though her voice is calm and low, "is he's using them as a battery or a booster. We learned many things while we were in Avalon, but he was far more interested than I. I'm afraid he may have perverted our hosts' magic."

Perverted some ancient beings' magic. Just fucking wonderful.

"I'm calling everyone in." I dare her to disagree but she nods instead. "I think we should head into the city, where we have access to modern technology." And plumbing, among other things, but I don't say that.

"I have a Jeep outside." I grin as she holds out the keys. "I can ward wherever we end up, like I did here."

So many things are starting to make sense now. This stone temple is her safe place, her hidey hole. I stare at her for a moment. She brought me here.

"You brought me here." She nods. "You knew the others would eventually end up knowing about this place. Why? You could have taken me anywhere to heal me."

"It is time for me to stop hiding." That's all she says before turning and walking to the entrance.

She glances back to see if I'm coming, so I nod and begin to follow. Once outside, I squint at the brightness of the sun. I've been inside that temple for weeks, first to heal and then doing some hiding of my own. After I woke, I stayed to try to connect with Citlali, afraid to leave just in case it was the place that allowed me to.

Whistling, I take in a beautiful, jacked up Jeep Renegade,

matte black with black wheels. The top is hard and the windows are almost completely blacked out. It has a Punisher sticker on the gas cap. I think I'm in love.

Sitara grins at my reaction. "I thought you might like it."

"I had something similar once." I think I hear her whisper 'I know' but I'm not sure. "This is yours?"

Her head shakes as she climbs in the passenger side. Hopping in the driver's seat, I wait for her to tell me whose it is, but she doesn't.

"Come on, whose is it?"

"I thought you would need a vehicle." My mouth falls open. She bought me a Jeep, a fucking cool ass Jeep.

"Why?" She shrugs, and I've been around her enough to know I'll get no other answer. "Okay." For now.

I make calls as I drive us down the mountain. Dagen and Charlie's place is big enough for all of us to meet. We arrive faster than I thought we would. I put the Jeep in park and turn the key off but stay in my seat.

She turns her body towards mine and looks at me, waiting for me to get the nerve to ask what I really want to know.

I feel like a child or a coward or both. "Arkyn?"

I glance at the house. Charlie is standing at the front window watching us.

"How long have you watched me?" Sitara draws a deep breath before letting it out slowly.

"Many lifetimes. I watched you fight for people that you no longer remembered were yours to care for." So, she knows of all my failures. "I watched their destruction almost break you, time and again."

"All my failures." Looking out the window, I try to make sense of it all, of her. "I led you to them." Climbing out, I slam the door hard enough to rock the vehicle.

Maybe, the biggest failure of all, I led a being of

immense power to my brothers. I stalk to the house, and Charlie opens the door with a frown on her face as she takes in my appearance or maybe she hears a difference in my song.

"You okay?" I give her a curt nod.

"Anyone else here yet?"

"Torryn and Lillian; they have a place just a few streets over. The others are coming. They were spread across South America." She doesn't need to say what they were doing.

We've all been desperate to find Citlali. For different reasons but all searching. I feel Sitara rather than hear her approach. I realize now that it's only because she lets me.

"Charlie, this is Sitara." Charlie smiles while pushing by me.

"I'm very happy to see you again." Again? "I knew you would keep him safe." She draws the woman into a tight hug before releasing her and turning back to me. "Sitara. I like it. I was tired of calling you 'the woman.'" They walk past me as I just stare at them. "You coming?" Charlie looks back over her shoulder at me after they get inside.

Following them, I try to figure out what just happened. "Anyone want to tell me how you know each other?"

"She is the one who took me from the parking garage, and I was the one that was with you when she came to take you." Her tone tacks on 'you idiot' to the end of her words.

"You knew she had me all along?" Now the look she throws my way is essentially... duh. "Well, excuse me, no one has said anything about that at all."

Now I sound like a huffy child so I push by them like one so I can find Dagen. I see him standing in the backyard talking to Evander. I'm surprised to see the boss man here. I know the others have been trying to keep him at the head office in New Orleans, since he's been so unpredictable since Grace was killed.

They both turn as I step through the patio door. I cross straight to them.

"It's very good to see you, Arkyn." Evander's eyes are bracketed by a new set of faint wrinkles, and I hate knowing I added to his burden.

"I'm sorry I caused such a ruckus." I glance back through the door at the women, their heads close as they talk quickly and quietly. "She could have gotten a message to you a lot sooner."

Luc appears, and I fight my instinct to tense. I hate when he or anyone does that shit.

"I think she might have had other worries." He's staring at Sitara as he speaks. I wasn't wrong when I thought he might be interested earlier.

"Maybe," I agree and then watching him, I add to the word, "Hell, maybe she was busy with her man."

He doesn't let me down. Of course, if I hadn't been looking for it, I wouldn't have seen the slight flex of his jaw muscles. Dagen raises a brow at me in silent question, and I shake my head.

No way will I be telling a soul that I think the King of Hell has a crush on the last of the Lumeria. Well, soon to be last, if I have anything to do with it.

I look between the two of them. The two most powerful beings left on this planet might just be the perfect match. She needs someone that can protect her. He needs someone that can see the real Lucifer.

"Do we know she's still alive?" The question pulls me from my plotting.

"Of course she's still alive," I growl at Evander. "He's keeping her for a reason. He wants Sitara."

"He's correct." I spin, looking at the woman in question. "He thinks I betrayed him. I suppose in a way I did."

36

"Not helping the Fallen wasn't a betrayal, Sitara." Her smile is filled with sadness.

"Thank you for trying to make me feel better, Arkyn, but Theon begged me to come with him, and I turned my back on him. I've hidden from him for thousands of years. I've heard him call for hundreds of times and I refused to answer." Tears pool in her strange eyes. "I created the monster he's become."

"No." Luc's voice is dark and filled with such rage that I turn to look at him. I feel his power fluctuate as he fights to control it. "My Father created the monster, just as He created the monsters that Theon is helping."

Evander steps closer to our leader. Laying his hand on Luc's shoulder, he leans close and whispers something low in his ear. Luc spins away, and his wings lift him into the air. I'm surprised by the speed of his ascent.

"Is he going to be okay?" Evander nods, but his eyes are locked on our fearless leader. "So you said you might have a way to find the girl and maybe get us ahead of the Fallen for once."

Okay, we're just going to ignore what just happened. Turning, I look back at Sitara, but her eyes are locked on Luc as he rockets away.

"Sitara?" She blinks and then lowers her face. She didn't hear his question. "Evander wants to know the plan. I thought you could explain it much better, since it is yours."

She explains her battery theory, adding her plan. I let my eyes drift up to the sky, wondering if we can do this without Luc.

"I think it will be enough with the Princes and the two descendants that have been found," she answers, before I even have a chance to ask the question or voice the concern.

"So, we just need to get them all here." She nods. "Charlie!"

The woman walks as slowly as she can, a smirk on her face. "Yes?"

"How far out is everyone?" She just looks at me. "Please."

"A couple hours at the most."

I look at Sitara, and she sees something in my face. It scares her.

"I'm going to kill him."

"If he doesn't kill you first."

CHAPTER 9

CITLALI

*S*till not dead or at least, not still dead. She has risen!
I chuckle at my own joke even while I run my hand over my chest and stomach.

He took his anger at Sitara out on me, but the stab wounds are gone now. Doesn't mean I can't still feel the pain of the blade going in over and over, so many times I lost count before I lost consciousness.

This time, I'm laying on a concrete floor. I glance around the space. Warehouse maybe. Pushing up to sit, I look at my legs and finally notice how thin they are.

I wonder when I last ate? I remember one day waking in a restaurant, but that seems like a lifetime ago. The doctor in me knows I've had to have eaten since then, but my body doesn't reflect that.

Trying to stand, I can feel how weak I've grown and I know this time is real. I'm really locked in this warehouse, starving to death.

I barely make it to the wall before I slide down it, unable to go any farther. Noise forces my eyes open, but I hadn't even realized they had closed.

True death is near in more ways than one. Theon stands inside a door at the other end of the huge room. He doesn't bother closing the door as he starts stalking my way.

I can feel his anger from here. Rage rolls off him like flood waters down the side of the mountain, an unstoppable force.

"Is this the day?" I ask, although it comes out lower than a whisper and my voice sounds like a dried husk.

He hears me though, I know, because his head cocks to the side slightly as he puzzles over the words.

"Is this the day I finally die for good?" This time I sound stronger as my own anger begins to take hold.

"Maybe." He shrugs as if it is of no consequence, and I suppose it isn't to him. "I was certain she would have shown herself by now."

"Maybe you overestimated my value." I glare up as he stops in front of me.

"I don't think so. It is more likely she is scared to die herself." His eyes narrow as some thought comes to him. "Or she's not as powerful as I thought."

I don't think the last is the case at all, even though I've never seen her use her powers, whatever they may be. He looks at me and frowns. A little hint of disgust flickers in his eyes, and I wonder what I must look like.

Glancing down, I see blood stains on my clothes, mixed with dirt and other things. I don't need to feel my hair to tell it is in mats, tangled and dirty.

"Sorry if I look unpleasant, but you haven't had me awake in a spa yet." I push as much disdain into my voice as I can muster.

He seems surprised by my show of defiance and then he smiles. "You're right. Where are my manners?" He makes a show of waving his hand, although I know now he has no need.

Suddenly, in the center of the room is a large sunken tub, and I can see the steam floating from the water filling it. The scent of jasmine and vanilla fills the air. Hundreds of plants appear and transform the warehouse into a jungle. Flowers line a path to the tub, and petals cover the floor.

He reaches for me, and I flinch back. "Let me help you." He sounds reasonable, and I feel the moment I break.

He smiles gently as I reach out for his hand, but I don't miss the hint of victory that shines in his face. This is just a different type of torture. He lifts me, ignoring the smell as he carries me to a lounge chair I hadn't seen before at the side of the enormous tub. It reminds me of the ancient tubs in Rome. Setting me down, he starts to remove my clothes, and I can't be bothered to feel shame.

I rely on my clinical brain, thinking of him viewing me naked in a medical setting.

I let him help me into the steaming water. It burns at first, but I enjoy the feeling, letting it remind me I'm still alive.

He sits on the lounger, watching as I let myself slowly sink below the surface. I blow my air out in a stream of bubbles so I slowly settle on the bottom. I stay there until my lungs burn like fire. When I break through the surface of the water, he is gone. A table has appeared, and it is loaded to the point of buckling with food and drink. I stare at it with longing but I can't talk myself into leaving the heat of the bath. The lip of the tub has jars filled with all kinds of soaps and shampoos. I fill my hand with one that smells like mint and rub it into my mangy hair. It will take hours to get the curls untangled, but first I focus on just getting it clean.

I let myself float on the surface as I rinse the soap out. I grab a handful of thick conditioning butter and work it through the long lengths before twisting it up on top. A clip sits near the products; he has thought of everything.

Grabbing a loofah, I dip it in a bowl of minty smelling

body wash and scrub every inch of my body before once again letting myself float to rinse my body. I keep my head out, wanting to let the conditioner do its work.

The water cools as I drag myself out of the tub. My exhaustion has reached a critical level but I manage to stumble to the lounger. Sitting, I reach for some bread and juice.

Even though I want to gobble everything, I know better. My body will rebel, rejecting the food after going without for so long. I chew slowly as I try to plan an escape. Unfortunately, I feel myself slipping into sleep or unconsciousness, depending on how you look at it.

'I'm out of time, Arkyn.'

I smile as once again I picture him in my mind. I try to imagine what his voice sounds like outside my head.

'Good thing we are coming then. Just stay with me, Lali, and I will find you.'

I startle at his voice. *'How?'*

'Sitara figured out how he's hiding you. How come he's so strong. We helped her do the same thing. We are coming, Gdab.' I don't know what he just called me, but his voice softened when he said it, so I'm going to assume it is something good.

I don't know how to tell him that it's too late.

CHAPTER 10

ARKYN

*H*er voice faded. Just slowly slipped away as she spoke. I glance at Sitara. She is sitting next to me in the SUV that Evander is steering through the maze of overcrowded city streets, and I'm glad they didn't hear me call her lover.

She shakes her head. Even though Citlali won't respond with the boost from her connecting us all, sipping at our powers and if how I feel is any hint, our life forces, I can still feel her.

"Left," I murmur as I close my eyes to focus, trusting Evander to keep us moving in the right direction.

We continue this way until we make our way out of the city and into a more industrial area. Large warehouses stand beside a busy port full of ships.

"How will we find her in all this?" I ask as Evander slows down. "I know she is within a few blocks but I can't seem to pinpoint it."

"It's my turn now. Keep connected to her. Stop the car, please." Evander does as she asks, and she squeezes my hand before stepping out. Turning, she locks eyes with me and says, "I most likely won't survive today, so keep her safe. Find the others. Ask Diniel for help if you need it; Lucifer will know of him. I'm certain your powers will grow as each couple is completed."

I start to argue, but she turns and fucking floats away. Floats. Lady has mad skills. Leaning over, I grab the handle and jerk the door closed.

"Where to?" Evander looks at me in the rearview, and I shake my head. I have no idea. "Let me get the others here. We can go building by building."

"No." I think that is a real bad idea. "I have a feeling that asshole will call in his friends if he feels like he might lose this fight with her. Or he'll kill Citlali before we can get to her." His fingers tap on the steering wheel. He's more impatient than I am, but I know he'll wait. He wouldn't do anything to risk losing one of the girls, doesn't want any of us to suffer the way he is.

I'm watching him as he stares out the window so I see the moment he stiffens. I follow his line of sight and throw myself across the backseat. I've never seen Sitara's brother, but there's no mistaking the man strolling down the street towards her as anything other than one of her people. He is simply more, and the stink of evil clogs the air around him.

"Stay in the vehicle, Arkyn. You heard her," Evander growls. "Don't make her sacrifice be for nothing."

I flinch at his words and tone, but he's right. So I stay, but my hand refuses to leave the handle. Somewhere along the way, I began to care about that woman. People I care about end up dead or enslaved.

She stops her forward motion and waits.

"Sitara, I was beginning to think I was wrong about you caring for the woman. But she literally stunk of your magic. The others didn't."

She remains silent.

"You figured out how I was finding them." He grins, and it is something straight out of Hell.

"You searched for my magic." Her voice is low.

"I did. It took me a while to find it with the angel's powers wrapped around it. Was that your idea?" She nods once, and he smiles bigger. "So you did pay attention to our hosts."

She nods again. And I can see his muscle twitch just under his eye; she's pushing at his buttons. He's so angry that he's left his soft underbelly wide open to her attack.

"You have nothing to say?" He takes a step forward.

Just as he does, I feel Citlali stronger as his control slips a tiny amount.

"Drive," I bark at Evander. He stomps the gas, and we rocket forward. "Head east. She's not far."

He turns down a side street, and the back of the vehicle fishtails as he drags his phone from his pocket. I close my eyes and focus on the woman. I hear him rattle off our general location to someone.

"Slow down." The car lurches as he takes his foot off the gas. "Stop!" My forehead slams into the seat back as he does exactly what I said. My eyes fly open, and I jerk the door handle, opening the door and jumping out.

Evander is out right after, leaving the engine running. I'm running toward a large warehouse and I hear his steps pounding right behind me. I grunt as I bounce off a magical barrier.

"Fuck." I hear a chuckle and look up to see Evander grinning, his hand held out. "Not funny."

"It was a little funny." My palm slaps against his, and he hauls me up.

"How do we get through it?" I tap my finger against it, and it feels like I punch a stone wall again. "We don't know her magic."

"True. Try to reach the woman again. Maybe she can get out… He might have only set the ward to keep us out."

I mull his words over; he could be right.

'Citlali!' I scream the word through our link.

I feel her jerk to awareness.

'Arkyn?'

"I got her." He nods and turns to watch our backs.

'I need you to come to me. I can't get in, but we are hoping you can maybe get out.'

'I'll try, Arkyn, but I'm so weak.' She didn't need to tell me that; I could hear it in her voice.

I feel my heart clench. What if we rescue her and we still lose her? Sitara has all but said Citlali is my destined descendant. I might lose my chance before I ever actually get it.

"We need to come up with a plan C and quickly." Evander looks at me hard. "I don't know if she has the strength to get out."

I try not to imagine what he might have done to her all these weeks. Nine weeks he has held her in this building or another just like it. He had her completely to himself to do whatever he wanted. It's sad that I hope he only hurt her as a punishment for his sister. I pray to the God that abandoned me long ago that he did nothing worse. It's little and selfish of me to think this way.

An almost sonic boom blasts me from my wallowing and I spin, looking the direction we drove from. Sitara. Luc appears in front of me, and I step back, gritting my teeth.

"Damn it, man, please stop doing that." He smiles. Shit, he does it on purpose. "Really?" He only shrugs.

I shake my head.

"Can you get us in?" Evander reminds us of why the man appeared in the first place.

Luc turns and places his hand a hair's breadth from the magical ward. His power rolls over the entire area. Evander and I both stumble under the force of it while squeezing our eyes shut to block out his blinding light as he completely blasts the ward.

The Morning Star turns night to day. I slit my eyes slightly and watch as he literally burns the ward away. The second it is gone, I'm pushing past him and rushing to the door, happy to stay upright this time.

I can hear Evander following close behind, but the light dies and darkness wraps around us in an instant. I glance back, and he's gone.

What the hell?

"I'm certain he went to aid Sitara." So I'm not the only one that noticed his interest.

"Citlali," I call out, hoping she will help us find her. Silence answers me. "What if we're too late?" I'm not really asking him but Evander answers.

"We'll reach her in time." He speeds up even as he says the words.

We split apart when we come to the end of the hall. A door flanks each side, and we turn to them with military precision. He goes right and I go left. I listen as he calls her name as my heart pounds and I race through the darkness.

I would have passed right by her if the moonlight hadn't highlighted her pale skin. Sliding to a stop, I fall to my knees at her side.

"Evander," I call and try to keep my voice steady.

I don't wait for him to reach me. Instead I pull my shirt over my head, covering her with it and hiding her emaciated body from his eyes. The monster had starved her. I want to rip him limb from limb or incinerate him with lightning. Maybe both at the same time.

I ease Lali into my arms, feeling stupid for calling her that in my head.

Sparks of electricity arc off my body, lighting up the room.

"Calm down, Arkyn."

I drop my gaze down in surprise, and caramel eyes meet mine for a split second before they close once more.

CHAPTER 11

CITLALI

*I*t's positively electric being in his arms.

I want to laugh but I think I'm really dying this time. I think this is all a delusion or another illusion created by Theon.

This is the one that will break me for good.

If this is Theon, he hasn't forgotten a thing. In the temple, Arkyn's scent had wrapped around my senses. It reminded me of my trip to the Pacific Northwest, old growth forest damp with rain. So different from the rainforest I grew up in but comforting all the same.

Home.

My brain jerks at the thought. Sitara and my people are home, not some strange man I know nothing about.

That's not exactly true, girl. You know he's important and you know he's trying to save you, I chastise myself.

Sitara left me with him, which is something she's never done. She's never asked anything of me other than for me to learn. She taught me ancient healing techniques, chants, and herbs she learned from around the world.

My thoughts slam to a stop. Ancient. Theon has power. I

am a doctor. I believe in science but I also know there are powers that humans can't understand. Sitara is his sister.

She didn't teach me things she learned, she taught me things she knew, she had taught me...magic. I think about how often I hum the chants under my breath during surgeries.

Have I been using magic all along?

I start singing the first chant she ever taught me. I feel Arkyn's heart beat out the drum, and my voice follows it. Just as I begin to repeat the first lines, something begins to happen.

Electricity begins to course through my body, an electricity that has a distinctly male essence. *'Arkyn.'*

'Lali?' I've never been called that by anyone but I like it. *'What's happening to us?'*

'Magic.' I don't know how else to explain it. I struggle, fighting my way from the darkness that holds me tight in its grasp.

I can hear a gasp and feel the sensation of falling.

"Catch him," a deep voice growls, and the falling stops. "What's going on?" The voice growls to whoever he's talking to.

"Arkyn?" Another voice this time. "Why are his powers going haywire?"

"I don't know, Torryn. Just help me get them to the SUV." Things become clear as I get closer to consciousness.

'Are you bewitching me, woman?' Even in my mind, I can hear his laughter.

'Maybe you are bewitching me.' I smile.

'You've taken over my powers, so I'm positive I'm not doing this.' His powers.

'Are you like Sitara?' He chuckles.

'Oh no, sweetheart, I'm nothing near as powerful as Sitara.' He doesn't elaborate, doesn't say what he is. *'If you ever wake up, I*

have a long story to tell you, but I need to see those beautiful candy-colored eyes first.'

'*Candy?*' I wait to hear what he says next.

'*Like liquid caramel, warm and sweet.*' I think my cheeks are pink. Can a person be embarrassed when they aren't even awake? The heat I feel says yes.

The whole time we had our silent conversation, I've continued to hum the chant for healing.

"You see this, right?" The one called Torryn asks. "Am I crazy? It does look like she's literally gaining weight right in front of our eyes, right?"

"I don't know what to think. Luc says take them to the temple, so I'm taking them to the temple." I can tell we are starting up the mountain as the car sways with the curves. Not too long and we'll be safe.

"She looks better, but he looks like shit," Torryn yells at the driver.

'*Am I hurting you?*' Nothing. '*Arkyn?*' No response.

I crash through the last barrier and sit straight up gasping. My eyes fly around the car, skipping over the startled looks of the other people and landing on Arkyn's ashen face.

I've killed him.

Drained him dry like a vampire.

CHAPTER 12

ARKYN

*F*inally, I didn't fail.

I let her take it all, everything I have to give her. Willingly going to the darkness for her.

My one and only success, and I'm okay with it being my last act. *Are you listening, God? If You are or if anyone else is, give her my power, give her whatever is in me that she needs to gain her legacy. Her destiny.*

I can hear them calling me. Drawing in a shallow breath, I smell the temple. They have brought me back. I wonder if I'm back on the altar? Her willing sacrifice.

"NO!" Her voice sounds different out loud. Deeper and husky, smoky even. It reminds me of a mixture of Macy Gray and Lauren Jauregui. I wonder if it's always like that or if emotion is changing it?

That's my last thought as power bows my back.

Hers maybe, Luc's for sure, and then the very feminine touch of Sitara. All three hit me with all they've got. Then I feel the lightning sliding through me, and I know it is her, for sure. She's giving it all back.

The others pull theirs back, and I can feel my head beginning to move back and forth as more and more courses through and over me.

I feel her fall onto me, her bones digging into me. I grasp her tightly, pulling her up with me.

"Stop, Lali, stop this. You are so much more important than I." Her hand comes up as she turns her face, and I see those caramel colored eyes bright with tears.

Cupping my jaw, she shakes her head. "You are everything."

I feel tears filling my own eyes at her words, even as my head shakes in denial. Movement causes me to glance beyond her, and I see Sitara smiling. She looks like something more than an angel, otherworldly maybe. Her hand comes up, and she quickly wipes away a tear that is running down her cheek.

Then she nods, and I see all of my brothers step up, along with Luc and the women. She begins to chant. Charlie steps closer, her hand reaching for my hand, and I let her take it as she starts with the beat she showed me in Las Vegas. My beat. The chant is in perfect rhythm with it.

Charlie leans close. Smiling down at both Lali and myself, she whispers low.

"It's her song." Tears run from the corner of my eyes, and Lillian and Charlie wipe them away. I feel the power of all these people running over us.

Lillian leans down, "No one, not us or even Him, ever thought you have failed."

Is she trying to make me look like a baby in front of my brothers? I'm a damn Prince of Hell and I'm laying here crying. Shit. I try to not make eye contact with any of them, but Luc draws near.

Nope, not you.

As soon as he steps near, the others follow suit with the women moving back giving them space.

It's Zeph who dares to speak. "We have all lost our charges, brother. Do you think badly of us because of it?" I refuse to answer him. "Are you going to make me find the answer?"

"Stay out of my head, Zeph," I growl.

No way am I letting him take a stroll through my head. Too many memories, things he and the others never need to know about. Sure they lost their charges at the beginning of this stupid war, but I've failed over and over.

Lali's fingers stroke over my cheek, and I focus back on her face. "No one could have saved them." I feel myself drawing away from her. She sees it on my face or maybe in my head. "I'm sorry. The connection, the magic, showed me." Tears fill her eyes. "I don't know how to stop it."

I try to relax, to ignore the fact that she has seen all of my shame, but I can't.

"Sitara, help me," she begs the woman. "I didn't know. You didn't explain."

I look at the woman in question, regret stamped all over her face. Her face turns to Luc, and she nods.

"Close your eyes, both of you," Luc cautions, and I do it but not before I watch him take Sitara's hand gently in his. "This may hurt."

Wonderful. Physical pain to go along with the emotional damage. I'm not prepared for her scream as he blasts us with his power, focused and multiplied by Sitara's magic. I grab her and squeeze her tightly to me, fighting when I feel her body moving away. "Let her go, Arkyn!" It's not Luc's voice, it is Lucifer's, and I realize he didn't have us close our eyes because of the light. It is because of what he didn't want us to see.

I feel more tears; he has freed his monster for me.

He is sacrificing what might have been to save me and Citlali. He has shown Sitara his face. The face of Satan that has terrified believers and non-believers alike since the day he was cast into Hell.

He was trying to shield the women, to keep them from looking at him differently.

I don't know if it is because of the strange connection with Lali or maybe I've just felt too much today, but he's killing me. I realize in that instant everything he's sacrificed for us.

I was already dead in the darkness when he fell for us and was cast into Hell for disagreeing with the Father. I've pieced together the story over the years, picking up things from Evander and those who were pulled out first. Those who chained the demons faster than I did heard more of the truth of his fall from grace. Since Lillian was found and then Charlie, I've seen him with them, his surprise at their acceptance, the stiffness when they embrace him, and now he's risking losing that which he's not felt in thousands of years. Hell, he probably didn't have either much before his disgrace, for being the favorite of the Lord wouldn't have made him many friends among those living in Heaven.

That was the Lord's mistake; He thought the angels couldn't possibly feel jealousy or anger.

He was wrong on both accounts. His hubris caused all of this.

Suddenly, I feel as if I'm being ripped apart and I can hear Lali's screams. Then it's like a rubber band that's been stretched so tight it snaps. She is jerked from me, both physically and mentally.

My body arches from the force of it, and when I open my eyes, I see my brothers flat on their backs on the floor. Only Luc and Sitara still stand, and I'm positive it's only because of their joined hands.

She slowly pulls her hand away, and I watch as he shuts

down, once again the aloof young man who seems so far above you that you don't bother even approaching him.

I glance around and I meet the sad eyes of Lillian and Charlie. They had seen the potential too.

Lali is laying on Victor, and while I'm glad he kept her from getting hurt, my demon growls in displeasure at him holding her against his body. He grins at the redness of my eyes.

"Come, kitten, we are poking the bear." His Russian accent is thick as he sits her up and to the side.

Lali looks up at me, still on the altar, her eyes fighting to focus. "Arkyn?" She frowns as her vision clears and she takes in my red eyes. "What?" She looks at Sitara as the woman steps around Luc. "Sitara, what is going on? Who are you? What are you?" She begins to scoot back even as she asks.

We've lost her.

CHAPTER 13

CITLALI

They are monsters.

He...his face. It was indescribable. Arkyn's eyes are still glowing red. The others just seem resigned. The women start towards me, but I shake my head and scoot even farther away.

I gather my muscles, trying to get my body under control. I had thought while we were connected that Arkyn was maybe the person I had longed for for so long, but it must have been the magic.

It twisted and hid his monster. All this time, Sitara had been...what? Her brother was insane, evil, and I had thought that she and Arkyn would save me from that evil. They did too, just to bring me to more, to greater.

Sitara draws near, but I shove up, spinning as I do, and race from the temple. I run and run, not caring where I go. Not paying attention to my surroundings. When I finally stop, I'm deep in the mountain jungle. Glancing down, I realize I'm in trouble in a single breath, a beat of my heart. I'm in the flimsy clothes Theon had left for me, no shoes, and blood is streaming from cuts on my feet and legs.

It's growing dark, and I'm lost in the rainforest, bleeding, a lure for predators.

I need to get the bleeding to stop. I look around and just up from me, I see the outline of something that makes my nerves calm slightly. Even in my mindless run, my subconscious took me to safety. There, hidden in the branches, is the old treehouse of the village elder, which means somewhere below it is the garden of plants and herbs she had so painstakingly transplanted and tended. Even though she has been gone for many years, they will still be here.

I stumble up the slope. Now that my adrenaline has crashed, the pain of the cuts pulses through my body. Luckily, it only takes me a few minutes to find yarrow. Pulling some, I drag myself up the rotting ladder into the safety of the trees.

Everything is how she left it, and I sigh with relief to find blankets and clothing. First I sit and tear some of the silk from a gown and crush the yarrow before wrapping my damaged feet gently.

Grabbing a blanket, I shake the layers of dirt from it before dragging it around my shaking body. I'm not cold.

I just keep picturing the face of the man that had held Sitara's hand. It was normal, like a very young man, and then when I opened my eyes a crack, a monster straight from a horror movie had stood there.

I will never get that image from my mind. Never.

What had Sitara raised me for?

"Citlali?" I know his voice and I freeze. If one finds me, all of them will. "Citlali? I won't come up but I know you're bleeding. Are you okay?"

He sounds so defeated, so heartbroken. I clench my teeth refusing to answer, to ease his worry.

My brain can't make sense of the man I connected with and the thing I saw.

"I told you it was a long story, that I would explain it all when we found you." I hold my breath. "Do you want to hear?"

Do I?

I want to scream no. To deny all of them, especially Sitara, who has raised me as a sacrifice to these monsters, but I saw him with all those tribes, felt his pain at their loss. How can someone feel that much pain and be a soulless monster?

Science says the two things can't coincide. My head and heart hurt. My heart wants to hear him out. My head is afraid that the connection has corrupted my heart.

"Are the other monsters coming?" I hate how scared those whispered words sound.

"No. Just you and me." I hate that he sounds even sadder, knowing that I caused it.

"Start at the beginning." I move closer to the ladder opening. "Wait." He glances up at me. "Start with me. Am I supposed to be sacrificed to all of you?"

He smiles sadly while shaking his head. That's good news, if he's telling the truth.

"Can you lie to me?" I blurt the question I'm thinking.

"No." What if he's lying now? This is stupid. I'm going round and round. Either I believe him or I don't. I must make a decision, at least where Arkyn is concerned.

Looking down, I see that he is staring out at the jungle, just waiting. He could have already been up here, killing me, raping me, doing God knows what, but he's just leaning against the trunk of the tree. Waiting. For me to decide whether he is trustworthy or not.

"What have you decided? Believe me or not?" His voice holds a bit of amusement, and I purse my lips.

"Okay, go ahead with your story." Something in me knows I can believe him. I need to hear all of this story. My story. His story.

"Our story, sweetheart," he whispers, but I can still hear him.

Our story. A part of me likes the sound of that, and I don't understand it.

He starts talking, his voice low but steady as an unbelievable tale begins to flow from his lips, lips that seem too rosy for a man. Listening while leaning against the same tree trunk, I let those words take me away to an amazing world.

Heaven is real. God is real. Angels are real, and it seems most are real dicks. Arkyn was an angel.

Arkyn was an angel. Arkyn is a demon. A Prince of Hell.

His voice dies away, and I glance down. "I guess you have reached my portion of this tale." His dark eyes meet mine, and he nods. "Don't hide anything from me. Tell me everything."

He does; he tells me everything.

Sitara had told me I was from a long line of healers. How could I have known it started with Raphael, an Archangel? I don't know what to say as once again, he falls silent.

Finally, he stands and looks up, waiting. I nod slowly, and he begins to climb up, pausing after each rung to give me the chance to change my mind.

Now, knowing everything, I see how honorable he is, has always been. His anguish at failing his people. My people.

I wonder if Raphael had something to do with his assignment to the First Peoples, if the healer that had fallen in love with one of them had hoped to protect them all through the ages?

"Who gave you your assignment in Heaven?" He looks up and stops on the ladder at my words.

His head shakes. "It came from above. That's all I know."

"Did you know Raphael?" He nods as he pulls himself into the treehouse.

"Not well, but I had met him on occasion before he was sent to Earth. Why?" It's my turn to shake my head as I shrug.

"Just wondered." I watch as he slides down the wall opposite me. "What of Sitara? Is she an angel?"

"No. She is the last, or at least we thought she was, of the Father's first creations. The Lumeria, destroyed by Him for their ambitions. They have powers, maybe ones even greater than ours."

I know I've only experienced a hint of the powers her brother had so I can't imagine the scope of what he hints at.

"The temple was built for her." I realize she had told me many times over the years it was hers but I never understood. "My people worshipped her as a goddess hundreds of years ago."

"Makes sense; her magic would have seemed very godlike."

"I think she has watched over my entire line." He nods. "Was she waiting for me?"

"Maybe. Or maybe she was waiting for us." His eyes lock on mine. "She seems to have been watching me for a very long time as well. Maybe she waited for us to find Lillian."

"Why?" He draws a deep breath and holds it for a minute. "So, there's more to this story."

He sighs, and a laugh is strangled in it a bit. "I'm afraid I've saved maybe the biggest part for last."

"Why?" I watch as his Adam's apple bobs.

"I don't want you to run. To lose you before..." He looks away.

"Before?"

He glances back at me, and I see hope flickering in his eyes but there is also worry there.

"Arkyn?" I wonder what could worry a demon.

The fact that I even have that strange thought proves what an insane world I'm now a part of.

"There was a prophecy written in Heaven after the war. It foretold of the descendants and how they would join with those that were slain that day along with the Archangels. Together they would defeat the Fallen."

"So, I'm supposed to fight with you." His eyes shift away, and I frown. So not fight. I play his words over in my head again. Oh. "Shit. You mean...like...biblically. Join."

I push up and pace away. He does nothing, just sits silently. I pace and pace until he finally stands. His movement stops me in my tracks. I feel like doing exactly what he says as he stands before me. Run. Flee. This is my one chance. I know he will let me go.

I know his heart, it is honorable, and he will release me from my role in this, if it is what I wish.

Freedom.

He would sacrifice the world for my freedom.

Even if it meant one more failure to etch into his soul.

CHAPTER 14

ARKYN

I smile softly, letting her know I understand. I'm surprised Lillian and Charlie came around so readily.

Maybe it's because they already knew the world was full of demons. Maybe not real ones, but they had known all about evil. Citlali had been sheltered from it all by Sitara.

Maybe that was her mistake. She had hidden the evil too well.

I don't blame her for leaving. Hell, I would if I could. Okay, I wouldn't but still I don't begrudge her the need to flee.

"It's alright, Lali. Go. I'll keep them busy and give you plenty of time to get far away." I can't stop myself from reaching out and tucking her glossy hair behind her ear.

"Why do you call me that?" She looks at me curiously.

"Do you know what your name means?" She shakes her head. "Shooting Star."

"I don't understand."

I don't either, I guess. "I don't know, just fitting some-how." She smiles.

S LAWRENCE

"So, about the nickname." I was hoping she would move on to something else.

"I just wanted… I mean, I just needed to feel like maybe, just maybe..." I stop before I embarrass myself and her.

She stares at me, and I watch as something in her face shifts. It softens, and she reaches up, taking my hand in hers. She grips my fingers tightly. A goodbye.

"I don't understand any of this, Arkyn, but I understand you." Frowning, I stare at her face, trying to understand what she's saying. "Can you take me back? I need to talk to Sitara." She surprises me with the request.

"Of course." I douse the tiny flame of hope that flares to life at her words before picking her up and cradling her in my arms. Two steps and I'm at the opening for the ladder.

She makes a little squeak of a noise when I step out. We land softly on the ground as I bend my knees to absorb the impact.

"Damn it, you scared me." She sounds a little ferocious, and I know I better hide my smile. "Don't ever do anything like that again."

Oh, I'm totally doing that again.

It only takes me a couple minutes to get us back to the temple. Zeph is standing in the clearing outside the door. He's surrounded by at least ten little kids, all clamoring at him. I stop just out of sight, and we watch as he picks up one after the other, spinning them in circles as their laughter fills the air.

Lali practically melts against me at the sight. What is it about a man with a child that is like catnip for women? I step out, and he immediately stops.

"Too late, we already saw you, Uncle Zeph." He shoos them away, but I don't miss the wink he throws a little girl whose eyes were filling with tears at her lost turn.

"Shut up, man." His words have none of the old fire in

64

them. Even before the war and our deaths, Zeph had been a warrior. He had been in the second tier of angels, a Power angel tasked with keeping evil from the Earth. He spins on his heel, and I get a glimpse of the old soldier.

He growls but keeps walking away when Lali whispers, "That was so cute." I grin as I start to follow him into the temple. "You can put me down now, you know that, right?"

"I know." I don't though. I carry her until we enter the main room.

Sitara spins when she hears us enter.

"Citlali." The relief and love in her voice is that of a mother. "I was afraid…" She doesn't have to finish. We all know. I had felt it also. Still feel it, if I'm honest.

"Can we have some privacy?" Citlali looks at each of us, one at a time.

One by one, the others file out until it is just the three of us. I'm reluctant to leave, but she nods at me and I know she won't leave without at least telling me.

I pull her to me, hugging her close and drawing the scent of her into my lungs so I can memorize it. She tightens her arms around me, and I feel desperate for a split second. I could run with her or keep her. It is a crazy thought, and I force myself to let her go.

Turning, I force myself away and follow the others without looking back. When I finally reach the large opening that marks the entrance, only Zeph is waiting.

"The others have gone to their homes or to the hotel." He looks up from his phone, stares at me for a minute, and then looks back down.

"Why did you stay?" I watch him closely. Zeph is a man of few words. Over the long years, I've learned to watch him for minute facial movements.

He shrugs, not looking up.

"Seriously, Zeph, why are you still here?" This time he

does look up while tucking his phone into his pocket, but not before I see what he was looking at. Children's swing sets and other playground equipment. I don't say a single word, which is very good for my health. "Why didn't you volunteer to keep Luc's new baby?"

I shouldn't have asked, if the frown is anything to go by.

He ignores it but draws a deep breath, I hope to calm himself.

"I've watched you." He locks his eyes on mine, and I feel like I always do when he's looked at me. "Throughout our entire existence here, I've watched you. You have tortured yourself better than any of the masters in Hell. You, Arkyn, are a good man. You were a good angel, and I know you. So I'm going to make sure you don't do something eternally stupid."

"Like what?" My back stiffens at his tone and words.

"Like let that girl run away and hide." Well, fuck.

I guess he does know me. I don't know what to say. I mean, he's right... I'm letting her go.

"She didn't know anything about this shit, man. She doesn't deserve to be shoved in the middle of this God damned war." I stalk away from him.

I can hear him following but I don't turn or stop until I'm deep in the jungle. Fingers dig into my shoulder, stopping me.

"Do you deserve it?" I can't look at him. "Do I? Does Luc?"

The last is my undoing. I want to weep at the injustice of our lives. We all sacrificed, we all lost so much, but Luc—he lost everything and sacrificed the most. The women are giving up everything to join this fight.

"Aren't they gaining just as much?" My eyes fly up. I hate when he does that shit. "Your face cannot hide your thoughts. Never has. I wasn't the only one who watched you.

Raphael and the other Archangels did as well. They saw great promise in you, Arkyn."

I look out into the jungle, hoping he can't see the emotions I'm sure are stamped on my stupid face.

"Awesome." The word breaks free as my anger and shame reach DEFCON level five.

"Why would that make you angry?" I spin and see genuine confusion on his face.

"Umm, I don't know, Zeph, maybe because I've been a failure my entire existence." He laughs, and I want to punch him in his stupid face. "Every fucking job I've been given. Whole fucking tribes were slaughtered because I didn't protect them. Men, women, and children butchered because I failed. I tried to save Uriel in Heaven, and Celine killed me."

I don't say how she tortured me before she finally let me die. I refuse to talk to anyone about it. In fact, only Luc knows the truth of that day.

"I was killed that day also. So were all our brothers. Are we all failures that deserve this eternal damnation?" He raises a brow, knowing he's beat me.

I will not damn my brothers.

"You can't let her leave. Show her your heart, Arkyn." I shake my head. "Do you think she wouldn't have seen your true nature when she connected to you? I heard her words as clearly as you. She said what when you tried to get her to let you die?"

Swallowing, I refuse to answer him.

"She said, 'you are everything'. Why would she say that if she had seen something so unworthy in your soul?" I shake my head.

"She was confused by the power she didn't know how to wield," I argue.

"Okay." I can hear him rolling his eyes.

"You were a warrior, still are, fought many battles and won. You wouldn't understand."

"I wouldn't understand failure?" He spins me with the skill of a seasoned fighter, and so much anger is radiating from him. "When the first Archangels fell, I went to my friend, my brother on the field, to help him, and she killed Raphael right in front of me. Then she killed me and she only knew how because I had trained her, fell for her lies about wanting to learn to bond with Raphael." He shoves me, and I stumble back, unprepared for his attack. "I taught Lina how to kill my best friend."

The last comes out as a battle cry, but this time I'm ready, or so I think. I've trained with Zeph for a thousand years but I realize after mere moments that he has been holding back the entire time.

His fists connect with my face multiple times in a second, and I feel blood flowing freely down my face, taste it in my mouth. Shit. I try to fight back, and he proceeds to kick my ass.

In minutes, I'm on the ground just trying to protect myself.

"Zeph." Luc's voice rings out just as I feel a hint of his power wrap around Zeph.

The man instantly calms, the red of his eyes fading slightly but it continues to pulse with his rage. He struggles against Luc's power, and I hear footsteps racing toward us. I pry open my swollen eyes and see the women running our way.

"No! Stay back." Neither listen. "Please, he's out of control." Sitara looks between me and Luc.

She veers to the left while Lali slides toward me in a move that would make any major leaguer proud.

"Oh, Arkyn, what did he do?" Her fingers feather over my face, the doctor taking over from the woman. She prods, gently searching and finding the multiple broken bones hiding under the swollen flesh.

I blink as a tear hits my cheek. She is crying for me.

"Lali, I will heal. Don't cry." She wipes at her cheek, and I see my blood smear across her tan skin.

"Why are you always hurt?" She mumbles.

"It is a talent of mine." I try to smile but end up wincing as I manage to split my lip even more.

"Yes, he's very good at getting his ass beat," Zeph growls. "He's very good at losing. I don't think he's actually ever won."

"Excuse me?" She pushes up, turning to face him. "Do not talk about him like that. He is a good man and he doesn't deserve you being vicious."

He laughs, and she kicks him right in his balls. Holy shit, she kicked him in the junk. I can't hold in the bark of laughter that bursts free from my throat.

Zeph crumbles to his knees.

"Damn, the mighty warrior brought to his knees by a girl." I laugh harder.

When he looks up, the red is gone, and I feel Luc draw back his power.

"Oh God, Arkyn." The man, my brother, crawls to me, his hand curving around my cheek, softly. "I'm sorry, brother, so sorry. I would never..." I see the shame in his almost-lavender eyes before he breaks free from Luc's grip and flees from us.

I struggle to my feet. Lali helps while making a noise that says she doesn't think I should move. Luc steps right in front of me and so does Sitara. They join hands and their combined powers flow through me. I grimace as my bones knit together much quicker than I'm used to.

Lali just stares as my face returns to normal. Her fingers

reach up and glide over my newly healed cheek as the flow of power from the others stops.

"I need to go after him." I look at her to make sure she understands. "He didn't mean to hurt me." I won't have her thinking badly of him, not after everything he had lost.

"You stay. I'll go." Luc glances between us before starting to step away.

I smile, my cheek moving under her palm, and she nods. Following Luc to the edge of the trees, I touch him lightly on his shoulder. His eyes meet mine as he glances back at me.

"Did you know about Lina?" Our leader sighs.

"I know everything, Arkyn." Jerking his head, he moves farther into the trees. "I know every tragic detail of that day. I know how tormented each of you are over events that have long been out of your control. I know that you all wrestle with more than the demon I put in you."

"Do you know why he lost control? I mean, I understand his anger, but Zeph wasn't there when he looked at me. Just his demon stared back at me." I had pushed him too far. "I shouldn't have teased him about the kids. I was feeling sorry for myself."

Luc stares up into the canopy, silent as the seconds tick by, and I grow more apprehensive. I fight the urge to pace.

"Zeph has…" He pauses and just that act has my hair standing on end. "Well, he has been, for lack of a better word, suppressing his true nature. He is an angel of battle, a Power made for battle, but since he began to walk this Earth as a demon, he has fought no battles."

"What? No way, that can't be right. We have all fought the Fallen." He shakes his head.

"He has tracked them but he has lifted no weapon in a thousand years. When his rage breaks free from his control, a battle fury takes control of even his demon. I've tried to convince him to kind of vent it. Like a pressure cooker." I raise my brow but he shakes his head. "I'll go after him. You stay here and talk to Citlali. You need to do like Zeph suggested. Let her know you, Arkyn."

I don't even ask how he knows what Zeph suggested. The man has some scary mad skills when he chooses to use them. He doesn't wait for the response I'm sure he knows isn't coming; instead he just disappears.

I'm left standing there alone with nothing but my emotions. Self-doubt eats away at me. How could she choose me? The sky begins to lighten before a sound drags me from my thoughts.

"Are you coming back?" I spin at her voice. "You've been gone a long time."

"I was thinking." I feel stupid for sounding so much like a child.

"Sitara explained more of the prophecy, more about the other descendants." She watches my face closely.

"You should walk away." I look back out at the trees. "Go save people, go be a doctor."

"So I should walk away and save a few but let the rest of the world die or worse?" She frowns.

"Yes, be selfish, for fuck's sake. You were already kidnapped by a madman who could have killed you any time he wanted." She smiles a little, just the slight curve of the corner of her lips.

"Arkyn." She sounds vaguely like a mother who has reached her limit with a kid. "From what I understand, that could happen to any of you, the other women...hell, the entire human race. I'm staying. I'm fighting."

"Did Sitara explain everything?" I emphasize the last word.

"She suggested I have you take me to see Charlie and Lillian." Oh, boy. I love those girls but I'm not sure Citlali is ready for them. "I'd like to talk to them, Arkyn."

I nod, turning back toward the temple. She falls in beside me, so I shorten my stride to match hers.

When we reach the edge of the trees, I see Lillian standing beside the Jeep waiting. I stop, and Citlali follows suit, standing at my side.

She looks up, turning to face me.

"I'll come back. I mean, how much more could there be?" She gives me a quick grin before jogging away to Lillian.

So much fucking more.

CHAPTER 15

*L*ooking back, I don't understand the look of turmoil on his face.

"I hope you have the answers I need." The woman nods as I jerk open the door to the Jeep. She opens the other door and looks in as I slam the door before I take Arkyn's advice and bolt.

Grabbing the seat belt, I'm about to pull it across my lap when she clears her throat.

"Sorry, but I don't drive. Until a few months ago, I was a prisoner of the Fallen." She shrugs.

My dramatic exit is less so when I have to climb over the stick shift into the driver's seat. She giggles and then runs around to the passenger side, and I shake my head.

My heart pounds as she looks at Arkyn. The love I see on her face stirs something in me. Jealousy? Longing?

The slamming door startles me. Blinking, I clear my thoughts and focus on her.

"Sorry, what?" I know she just said something to me.

"I said, Torryn has promised to teach me, but, and you can't tell him this, I really want Dagen to." She winks at the last, and I wonder if she realizes I really don't know who she's talking about. "I'm Lillian, by the way, if Arkyn didn't tell you."

"Citlali." Turning the key, I start the engine and pull onto the worn path that takes us to the actual road. "I didn't give him a chance. I was afraid I'd lose my nerve."

"Luc didn't say why you wanted to talk, but I can imagine." Can she? Who is Luc? The thoughts ping through my brain.

"I don't know who any of those people are." I smile to try to soften the tone of my voice.

"Oh, yeah, I forgot you were taken before you could meet all of us. It's been kinda crazy with the search for you, the Fallen, and of course, Arkyn before we found him here at the temple." As we reach the bottom of the mountain, she points to the right and I head into the city. "We rented a place near the beach."

I follow her directions through the traffic until we are in front of a beautiful beach home on the side of a hill. It's twice, maybe three times, the size of my home.

"Oh yeah, having a thousand years to build wealth has allowed them to become ridiculously rich." I'd say. "They all own parts of the company but they all give it all away, although they all think the others don't know. Silly men."

Philanthropist demons. It's like I'm in some crazy alternate universe. Angels are the real demons, and it seems demons are angels.

Arkyn's face pops into my mind.

"You coming?" She's already out of the Jeep but with the door open watching me.

The front door opens, a young man waves at us, and Lillian waves back. I wonder which demon this is.

As we draw near, Lillian grabs my hand and pulls me right in front of the man.

"Lali... I can call you Lali like Arkyn does, right?" I nod. "Great. Lali, this is Charlie."

Charlie is the name of one of the women Sitara told me to talk to.

"Hi." The voice is decidedly feminine. "I take it no one told you." I shake my head even as I smile and thrust my hand out at him or her, whichever... It makes no difference to me. Charlie smiles back, and this time it is genuine. I think I just passed some test.

"So, I ordered food, and everything is ready for a girl's night or day." I haven't had one of those since pre-med and I feel like this won't be anything like the last one.

Hours later, I'm sitting beside the pool, watching the sun set over the waves, and trying to not freak completely out. Both women stand at my side, one on the left and one on the right, and they are currently putting two very real sets of wings away.

The doctor in me wonders at the physical part of that—like where do they go, how do they do it? The human part of me is holding on by a thread, one that is slowly unraveling.

Lillian is the descendant of Michael, Charlie comes from Gabriel, and Raphael fathered my line. His genetics run through my veins; his DNA is part of my strand. My eyes slide right and then left. They have the DNA of angels in them also.

"If I asked for some things, could you or someone get them for me?" They look at each other then both shrug while nodding.

"Most likely. If we can't or Arkyn and the others can't, then Luc can for sure." Charlie nods again at Lillian's response.

Luc. Luc. Luc. No matter how many ways I change the emphasis, it still means the same thing. Satan, King of Hell,

Beelzebub, the Devil. Lucifer. His face in the temple flashes in front of me, and I jerk back against the chair.

"Are you okay?" Charlie drags another chair close and sits, leaning toward me. She has wings of fire. FIRE. "Did I tell you about my other… gift?" I shake my head. "I hear music for each of you—Torryn, Lillian, Arkyn, all of them, even Luc."

"Especially Luc." Lillian smiles and it is filled with love. Love for the devil.

"You have music too." Charlie draws my gaze back to her with her words. "I've been trying to record the different parts. Luckily, Dagen plays a lot of instruments."

Lillian giggles, "Like fate or something." I get it; they believe God created us for each other.

They believe I was meant for Arkyn. I don't hate the idea. I won't deny my attraction, my connection. Thinking about it, I suddenly get a flash of a memory. Not one of my own. Arkyn. He's talking to the one that beat him so badly. He's arguing about why would or how could I love a man who is nothing but a failure. My heart aches for him.

Then it is gone. My phone vibrates in my pocket. Pulling it out, I see a number I don't recognize and four words.

'Do you need me?'

He had felt me, and his only concern was if I was alright. 'I'm alright.' I respond but I stare at his words long after I send the message.

"He's the sweetest out of all of them." Lillian is looking down at my phone and then looks up, locking eyes with me. I see the warning. Don't hurt him.

"The most broken, I think." Charlie is looking out at the mountain. "He lost the most maybe, besides Luc. Over and over, he lost and even without his memories, he blamed himself. It broke him." She turns her head and pins me with a look. "Are you going to break him even more?"

How do I respond? I don't want to, of course, but I have no idea what I'm going to do.

"How long did it take you to decide to do this? To join this war?" I avoid the real question I want to ask.

"I chose Torryn, I think, the second time I spoke to him, if I'm honest." Lillian looks beyond me to Charlie. "He sacrificed himself to save me. Lucky for me, Luc saved the crazy man."

"I smelt Dagen and I think that was it." Charlie laughs when she sees my face. "The man smells like chocolate and of course, he almost died multiple times for me."

So they both knew, like, immediately.

"Maybe we should call Evander and have him bring the other guys over." Charlie looks at Lillian and then back at me. "I mean, we think maybe Arkyn is the guy for you, but Lillian, even you met everyone." She holds up her hand when Lillian starts to protest. "I know you were just kidding. Dagen told me he loved the look on Torryn's face when you asked. But maybe Arkyn is meant for someone else, someone who will protect him."

Lillian nods and takes out her phone while I start to get angry.

"True, he needs someone to heal him." Heal him. Heal. I'm a fucking doctor.

I HEAL people.

"Hey, Bossman. Can you get Victor, Drayce, and Zeph to come on over here? We might have been totally off." Lillian stands and paces away, her voice dropping. "No. Charlie and I both agree we won't let him be hurt."

Jumping up, I stalk to her, and she turns slowly. "Hold on, Evander."

"I wouldn't hurt him. I'm not going to hurt him." I spin away and jerk my phone back out.

I'm going home. Please meet me.' I hit send because I don't know what exactly I want him to do. I don't stop walking until I jerk the door of the Jeep open. As I back out of the driveway, I see the two women watching from the door I left standing open.

* * *

I GRIN at Lillian and she grins back. It was almost too easy. Citlali is tough and strong, just the kind of woman Arkyn needs to heal his heart and soul.

"Oh, shit." I look at Lillian again as the headlights race away.

"What?"

She shakes her head as she responds, "We didn't tell her about how we got our wings or about how the guys got theirs."

"Surprise." We both start laughing and have tears streaming from it when both Torryn and Dagen land in front of us.

"What did you do?" Soon their laughter fills the air.

CHAPTER 16

ARKYN

*S*he is pissed.

I can feel my anger rising at the thought of them hurting her. Luc and Zeph are standing beside me when the text comes through.

"I need to get to her house. To her." I'm shaking and I can feel my demon forcing his way forward to help me protect her.

"I can take you there," Luc offers, soothing my demon only slightly.

"I felt her." My hand rubs over my chest.

"Let me help you. Help her." I nod as I reach for his outstretched hand.

"This is it, brother. She is reaching out to you." Zeph wraps his arms around me and squeezes me, an apology and reassurance. "Let her in." He steps back as quickly as he moved forward.

I don't say anything. Luc nods at Zeph, who makes his way to the entrance, and I realize he has been left to protect Sitara.

Traveling through the world with Luc is an amazing privilege few have experienced. I watch atoms and molecules slip by us, marveling at the wonder of it all.

'She was created for you, Arkyn. If you let her, she can heal your soul.'

My jaw clenches at his words.

'Did you know that even your demon is different from the others?' Frowning, I try to focus on him, but we are nothing, just parts of the universe. Then just as suddenly as we came apart, we are whole again and standing in front of a cute little home that screams Lali. Tidy, well-groomed flower beds frame the front door.

"How is the demon different?" He sighs but smiles at the question.

"Do you ever feel the others' demons?" I try to think of the others. Of course I have but I guess I've never really paid attention.

"I mean yes, but they all feel powerful and not evil but angry. So angry." He nods.

"And yours?" I shrug, he feels the same to me. "Yours was so different. I felt him before I filled him with your essence. I knew you in Heaven, Arkyn. You have always been a gentle soul, even among the angels, and yet you raced to try to save Archangels. You tried to fight. You went up against someone you knew would kill you." He pauses, looking at my face.

I don't deny it. I've always been weak.

"That isn't weakness, Arkyn. That's the definition of courage." I disagree, but it's stupid to argue with the Devil. "Your demon was the same—not as powerful but willing to battle anyone or anything to protect people. He's a little broken like you, and Lali can help you both. If you let her."

I'm about to respond, but then he's gone. Poof. I'm staring into empty space when the night is lit up by headlights.

I can see her face through the windshield as she stops and

shuts off the engine. She doesn't move, and neither do I. I will stand here as long as she needs me to.

The night is filled with noise; birds calling to one another, bugs searching for food, traffic in the streets just a short distance away, and the barks of dogs, but even with all of the cacophony, I hear her drag in a deep breath.

She releases it slowly, and I brace myself for her decision. I memorize every curve and line of her body as she opens the door and climbs from the vehicle. Her long nimble fingers nervously play over the keys before she shoves them in her pocket. The fingers on her other hand fidget with her wild hair before tucking some of the strands behind her ear, and then she finally looks at my face.

I memorize the gold and surprising flecks of green sprinkled in their darkness. She doesn't blink. Instead Lali seems to be doing the exact thing I am.

I watch as something flickers in those unique eyes, some emotions I can't quite puzzle out.

I'm still trying when she strides forward, moving faster than I'm expecting until she practically slides to a stop in front of me. Our breaths mingle due to our closeness.

I'm frozen, paralyzed by her nearness. Then those beautiful fingers reach up and curve around my cheeks.

"You don't need anyone else." I have no idea what she's talking about but I can hear the anger threaded through her voice. "I'm a healer."

"I know," I whisper, still completely confused.

She surprises me again when she crashes into me. It is no soft tender kiss; it is quite simply a claiming.

Something inside me breaks wide open.

Claimed. Chosen. Worthy.

My eyes fill with tears, tears that have been held at bay for hundreds of years, hell, maybe my entire existence.

She kisses me deeper, exploring my lips and the dark heat

of my mouth. I do the same, tasting and savoring the flavor of her.

She reminds me of a chocolate I tasted in a small southern village in Mexico. It was rich with a subtle spice that exploded on my tongue.

I liked it so much, I have it shipped to my home but now, well, now I can have her instead. My hands find their way into her curls, trying to pull her even closer. Breaking away from me, she drags in a breath as I fight for mine.

"I had to know." I wonder what. "They said you needed someone else. That I should meet the others."

"The girls?" She nods.

"But I don't want to. Do you?" My mind is stuck on the image of her meeting the others. "I connected to you. Just you. That means something, doesn't it?"

"I hope so." I hate that I can't just say what I'm thinking.

I want to say no, you can't meet them. You are mine. Mine alone. Created for me. My fear eats at me though, and I remain silent.

"Do you need me, Arkyn?" She peers into my eyes, looking for my answer.

Her face softens even after my silence lingers. I can't imagine what she saw. Need. Desire. Longing. Or was it worse?

Hope.

Fingers slide down my neck, over my shoulder, and keep going until they thread through my own.

I let her lead me inside in a fog because my brain doesn't seem to be working properly.

Not until the clicking sound of the lock echoes in the dark silence of her home. That sound jump-starts my thoughts.

"Lali?" She's leaning against the door just watching me,

waiting once again. "What? I mean, did they tell you everything?"

"You mean about my choice?" I nod once, fear skating down my spine. "I thought that's what I just did."

No nonsense surgeon. Breath rushes from my lungs.

"Are you sure?" She smiles. It's the smile all women have, secret knowledge of their power hidden in it. Men should both fear and work endlessly for it.

"Zeph wasn't wrong, Arkyn. I saw the truth of you when you stayed with me while Theon had me and I was lost in his nightmare. You are a beautiful man, inside and out."

"I don't think I agree with that." She frowns, stepping forward.

Her fingers close around one of my braids, tightening as she steps around me. She pulls it firmly, leading me down a dark hallway.

Her voice floats back, and I feel my lips start to curve into a grin. "I will just have to change your mind."

"How do you plan to do that?" That secret smile peeks through her hair as she glances back at me.

"Let me show you." She pulls me farther into the room. Turning me, she starts to back me towards the bed, shoving me the last few feet so that I end up falling back on the over-stuffed mattress. The velvet is warm and soft under my hands. "Take off your shirt, Arkyn."

Sitting up, I grab the edge of the t-shirt and drag it up over my head. She just drinks me in as I hold my breath, trying to forget that while I'm not a virgin, it has been a while.

She steps toward me and I can't seem to keep my mouth shut. "I...well... I mean..." She smiles as I pause. "It's just that it's been a while." I close my eyes. Jeez, I really am a girl.

"How long is a while? Because it's been a while for me as

well." She continues forward, climbing up onto my lap. "I mean I've not been with anyone since my ex, and that was…" She rolls her eyes back, thinking. "Nine months ago." She shrugs.

Nine months. I want to both laugh and cry at the same time. Fuck. Nine months is a blink of an eye. Do I answer her with the truth?

"Spill." She laughs a little even as she leans forward and kisses me along my neck.

Leaning back, she stares at me when I don't speak. Okay, I refuse to start this with a lie.

"It's been a bit longer for me." She waits, giving me time to gather my courage while doing calculations in my head. "Seven hundred sixty-three days."

Her eyes widen, and then I see excitement. Excitement.

"Seven hundred sixty-three days exactly," she murmurs.

"Not that I've been counting." She smiles bigger, and it is like a sunrise, as cheesy as that sounds. She literally lights up the room with her happiness.

"Is there a reason?" I don't want to tell her the real reason so I just shake my head. I can tell by the slight narrowing of her eyes she doesn't believe me, but she lets it go. "Well, good, because I have plans for you."

"Really?"

"Yes." One word and then she's pulling her own shirt over her head.

She's beautiful.

Perfect.

She's curvy with a classic hourglass shape, full breasts and hips that flare out. Her body begs for my touch, but when I lift my hand, it's shaking.

Have you ever wanted something so bad it terrifies you? She is everything, more than I could've hoped for. More than I deserve. She takes my hand, bringing it to the lilac lace and satin that covers one perfect breast. I feel the nipple harden under my palm.

The way I want her is savage and primal, and yet I only want to be tender and gentle.

I bend my head close and taste her skin as I let my hand begin to roam. My head raises to check her reactions, and she is smiling that smile. I take it as an invitation to continue. I flick my tongue over the pulse that's pounding in her throat, tasting her arousal. My body hardens in response, and it draws a moan from her as she shifts her hips against me.

The movement makes me feel suddenly aggressive, and I pull her to me. I lick my way down the valley between her breasts, lifting her body up, holding her off my lap as I fight the urge to devour her.

Her fingers wrap around my braids, sliding down until she reaches the bands that hold them. Plucking them off, she begins to undo them.

Rarely is my hair free, but I long to feel her fingers in it. She doesn't disappoint me. Her short, blunt nails scratch along my scalp and goosebumps skate across my skin. Those fingers pull my head tighter against her flesh. Pushing the fabric down, I suck her hardened peak into my mouth, rolling it between my teeth, testing to see what amount of pressure she wants or needs.

Her back arches when I apply even more. The movement pulls her free of my mouth, and she uses her hands to jerk my head back. Something in me comes alive at her show of power and dominance. I feel my demon perk up, feel him looking out at her.

She pauses, keeping my head bent back as she stares into my red eyes.

"I know you won't hurt me. But do you know that I won't hurt you?" I nod. "You do? I wonder." She jerks on my hair, and I let her fall back onto my lap. She pulls until I'm flat on my back on her bed. Her hands leave my hair and slide along the velvet cover until they close over my own hands.

She watches me as she drags them up over my head. "Do you trust me?"

I feel one moment of panic, mind flashing to punishments my demon received in Hell. *'Do you trust me?'* I ask him. I feel him start to calm. I nod at her and hold still as she ties my wrists with a black silken rope.

The fact that she has it there waiting gives me and the demon a rush of jealousy.

"There are things they didn't know about me. Things you didn't see during our connection. I'm a dominant. I need the control. Does it bother you?" I shake my head. "I think we will fit perfectly."

"Why?"

"Because I can give you exactly what you need. I can show you exactly how worthy you are." I blink. "I will worship you in a way you've never imagined."

My body throbs at the thought, and the demon practically purrs. We both understand this is her showing us something important. She sees us as we are, she sees how broken we've become, and she still finds us worthy.

My body that I didn't realize was straining against the bonds relaxes.

She once again reaches above me for something, and her face coming close is the last thing I see as she covers my eyes. I know and she knows I could get free, but that's the point, isn't it? Trust.

I let my eyes close behind the cloth, ready.

Time to let her start to heal my broken pieces.

CHAPTER 17

I memorize the faith in his dark eyes before I cover them.

I had told him I was dominant and I can be, but it's not a must. The rope and fabric are left over from my last relationship.

Before I went into surgery, I had thought I might try mental health but I grew too attached to my patients.

He needs this more than I. The restraint, the darkness. The deprivation shutting down the self-doubt that was filling every molecule of his being.

It will be my life's mission to show him how worthy and deserving of love he is.

I kiss along his jaw, avoiding his lips for now, moving lower and lower, stopping at the waist of his faded jeans. The muscles in his stomach twitch, and he makes a small sound in the back of his throat as I unbutton then slide the zipper down.

I let my breath whisper over him as I stare; the length of his dick is impressive. My tongue licks over my bottom lip as I imagine it filling me.

Sliding off him completely, I work the pants off until he is lying completely bare before me. Stripping off my own clothes, I watch as he fights to remain still, even as his head tilts slightly as he tries to pinpoint my exact location.

I can't help but stare at his perfection. He's slim but solid muscle, abs for days, and those deep cuts at his hips. He is the most handsome native man I've ever seen, and I've been surrounded by them my whole life. I wonder for a moment if he was created this way or if he chose to look like those he couldn't save. The thought makes me want to weep, because I know the answer deep in my heart. Another punishment for another failure in his eyes.

Pushing the thought away, I step to the edge of the bed and let my fingers feather over his leg, working my way up.

I'm the healer and I will mend his broken pieces, and it starts right now.

I close my fingers around the long length of him, reveling in the hot velvet feel of him and the glistening moisture on the tip. Mouthwatering.

Holding it up, I begin to lower myself to the hard flesh. My hair slides over his thighs then higher over his stomach, and again he makes a noise, although this time it's deeper, more animal-like.

My tongue flicks out, catching the pearled drop. The taste explodes over my tongue, and it's my turn to moan. I hear the rope stretching as that moan vibrates over him.

So much power. I hold it all, and it is as addicting as he is. Grinning, I begin to devour him, slowly licking, kissing, and nibbling over every inch before making my way back to the top.

I draw him into my mouth, sliding slowly until he bumps the back of my throat. All the while, my hand is working, circling the part that won't fit.

Over and over, up and down, slow then fast.

"Lali." A plea.

I respond by taking him as deep as I can while applying pressure, pushing him closer and closer. I watch his body, his muscles tightening as he fights. His head moves side to side.

All the while, I can feel his pleasure, and just underneath is the thought that he doesn't deserve what is coming.

I push further as I reach up and pull the blindfold from his eyes, letting him see the pleasure I feel at having him.

I lock my eyes on his as I draw him deeper, feeling my throat convulse around him.

I worship him with my mouth. His body tightens even more as his hips thrust up, and I smile around him. Finally. Finally, he believes me.

Thrusting harder, forcing himself even deeper, he keeps his hips flexed, holding himself deep within the heat of my mouth. I swirl my tongue over the underside, and it is his undoing. He roars, and I let my eyes fall closed as his hot seed fills my mouth. I swallow as I hear the rope rip apart.

I glance up just as his hands close over my arms. He drags me up and over him. Wiping the pad of my thumb over the corner of my mouth, I smile. He growls. Red flickers in his eyes, and I realize I've freed them both.

That's my last thought as he flips us. I catch myself on my arms as he pulls my ass into the air. Oh yes. His hand tightens on my hair as he pushes my head down. Fuck.

A finger glides through my folds. Soaked. Another growl is my only warning. He's hard already. Magic. Angel. Demon.

Thank you, God. I might go to Hell for that thought alone. He presses into me and grabs my hip with the hand free of my hair, pulling me back as he slams forward.

I muffle my scream in the velvet that now smells of him. I'm frantic, pushing back as he pounds forward. I ride him hard as he drives me higher and higher. Releasing my hip, he trusts me to continue my backward thrusts. That hand is everywhere—between my legs, on my breast squeezing my nipple hard, pushing the pain while a fierce pleasure begins to spiral out of control.

I'm chanting. More. Harder. Please.

He complies as he curves over me, his fingers playing over my swollen nub, and as I feel my body begin to break apart, long teeth sink into my shoulder, and I explode. I think I can see the birth of the universe. Stars and planets streak by. He comes again, my name on his lips.

We collapse, and he pulls me against him, still locked in me. I look back, and his lips caress over mine gently.

"I love you." I blink at the words.

I see him breaking apart as he pulls away, sitting up.

I've done exactly what they said I would.

CHAPTER 18

I love you. I just said that out loud and I mean it, but the look on her face says the words surprised her. Shock wiped the look of satisfaction that had been shining in her eyes completely away.

Eradicated it.

My heart stutters, but I'm not surprised she doesn't feel the same. Releasing her, I sit up but I force myself to turn and watch her. Something miraculous begins to happen. As I watch her catch her breath, her face softens and her eyes fill with tears.

Pulling herself up, she stops when her face, her lips are a whisper away from mine. Our breaths intermingle as we watch each other.

"Why are you crying? I'm sorry."

She shakes her head.

"Arkyn, do you believe in the whole soulmate thing?"

I don't know what to say. I want to believe. If it's true, it means she is mine.

"I do because the second you connected with me, I saw your soul and I think mine recognized yours. I don't know how this works or how I could love you without even knowing the little things but I know… I know in my heart that you are mine and I am yours."

My heart actually stops at her words. They are more than my I love you; they are a declaration, a choice, and as I feel something settle inside me, I watch as her eyes widen. That widening is my first hint that something big is happening. It happens in a flash of light. Glorious, silver wings erupt from her shoulders.

"Oh my God!" She grabs at me, the weight of them throwing her off balance.

I smile and I think maybe it is the first one that is real in hundreds of years. A sense of joy fills me. I don't know if I've ever felt this type of happiness.

Those shining silver wings wrap around me as I realize she has been connected with my soul this whole time. Something happens as they close around us.

Tears glide down her cheeks. They glisten like diamonds, and I can't look away from them.

'Pretty.' The gravelly voice of the demon whispers, and I agree they are.

"Aren't they though?" My brows draw down at her words. "Did you hear him?"

She nods, like it's something that happens all the time.

It's not. As far as I know, no one can hear him but me.

Warmth begins to spread through me, like it did when I tasted her blood. I still can't believe I bit her and she didn't seem to care. She, if I'm honest, seemed to like it.

"Oh, I did." I blink. "I'm still in here." She taps my head while laying her other palm over my heart.

And just like that, I can feel her there and I follow the feel of her right back to her. I let my mind connect with hers again.

Love. Love shines as brightly as her wings.

I look up at her eyes, and she is once again wearing that smile. I think I will never tire of it.

"I will spend eternity proving just how much I deserve you," I whisper against her lips.

"Do you believe that you do?" Once again, I let myself connect with her and look at myself through her eyes. I don't recognize the man she sees. "Maybe not completely, not yet, but..."

I pause, trying to think of the words, words that explain that for her I will be better, I will believe. Her eyes widen, I shift back a bit, and then I feel them.

Tears stream down my face instantly as I flex them. So long. So very long.

"Are they black?" I don't dare look back. Not yet. She shakes her head. Wait, what? I jerk my head right and peer behind me. They are silver like hers but mercury, dark with black tips. "I don't understand."

I told you, Arkyn. You are so very special. Always have been and it seems always will be,' Luc's voice whispers through my mind.

Standing, I pull them around me, inspecting them, letting my fingers glide over the stiff but still incredible softness of them.

The warmth and sense of wellbeing I had felt while cocooned within Lali's fades, but I feel different, deep inside.

I stay here hidden within the feathers as I try to figure this out. Everyone has black wings now, Torryn and Dagen both. Why are mine different? Special. That word can have so many meanings.

I hear her stand. Peeking through a tiny opening, I watch as she learns to balance, even as I drink in the sight of her gloriously naked with those magnificent glistening wings arched so high behind her that they are rubbing on the ceiling. Even as I notice, she looks up, and I stifle a laugh at her completely exasperated expression.

"The others had to go to Heaven to learn about their wings, but maybe you can learn from them," I offer as I tuck my own away. I'll worry about their appearance later.

"Heaven?" She practically yells.

I've apparently found her breaking point. Her breaths speed up, and I watch as sweat forms on her face. Panic. Sheer panic twists her face. Fuck. I reach for her, but she stumbles back. Spinning, I look for my pants and see them in a corner where she had tossed them earlier.

Grabbing them up, I fumble for my phone in my pocket then hit Dagen's number.

He answers on the first ring. Had they all been waiting to see if I screwed up? I push the thought away.

"I need help. She's scared. Panicked." I vaguely hear his response before I drop the phone.

Something is happening. Something bad.

"Luc!" I scream, knowing he will hear.

He appears, looking at me, his face rippling as he fights to keep his power under control. Upset, worried, ready to kill. For me. I feel something I can't quite understand. Suddenly, he turns and looks at her, and I feel a growl rumble up from deep within me.

She stands there naked, bared to him, and I hate it. Hate him for a second, afraid she will change her mind about choosing me. Lightning crashes to the ground outside. He shakes his head, and a long, flowing dress appears on her. It's lilac. My eyes narrow as I wonder about his color choice.

"For fuck's sake, Arkyn, do you want my help or not?" His hand whips out, and one long finger points at the chair, where her lilac bra and underwear lay. I'm an asshole.

"Of course. I'm sorry. I'm a complete dick." I finish then spin around as a door crashes open somewhere in the house.

"It's the others." He doesn't turn. Instead he steps toward her, and she makes an awful sound that draws my attention to her face. It flashes to something else.

"What the fuck?" Dagen's voice is overly loud in the bedroom.

"Ugh, it smells like sex and death in here," Torryn mumbles, just before he makes a choked sound. I glance back and see Lillian glaring at him and shaking her head. I think he might have Tourette's.

I look back at her. Her face is flashing between her own and the other. It's like her flesh became translucent.

Luc takes another step. She turns her head and focuses her now fiery eyes on him. Eyes set in a skull glare out at him even as she still fights for breath.

Power hits us like a shock wave as she loses total control. It knocks us to our knees, and even Luc stumbles back. In seconds, I understand her new powers.

Healers can kill.

She can give life or take it away.

Luc looks back at us, and we must look like fucking shit, because I see something I've never seen in his eyes.

Fear.

Refocusing on the Angel of Death standing in the corner like a dark queen, he calls out to her, "Citlali."

Nothing. No response.

A wet cough fills the silence, and I look behind me. Oh God no. Lillian is staring down at her blood covered hand. Torryn has a stricken look on his face just before his demon takes over, grabbing the woman and lifting her into his arms. He forces himself to his feet and stumbles from the room. I hope he doesn't stop until he's far from here.

I lock eyes with Dagen. "Go. Run, you idiot. Take her and get free from here." As he shakes his head, blood runs down from his ear.

Charlie screams, grabbing at him and dragging him from the room even as I watch red tears start to track down her cheeks.

"Lali!" I yell at her, trying to get her attention to focus on me, praying she lets them go. Images of whole tribes dying from smallpox and tuberculosis play on a loop in my head as I begin to cough. "Luc," I call out to him. "Luc." His head turns back to me. "Go. Before it's too late." He starts to shake his head but whatever he sees stops him. He turns, but not before I see the first trickle of blood running from his nose. "Hurry."

She watches him go, eyes blazing.

A deep wracking cough takes hold, and blood sprays from my lips, dotting the floor in front of her feet as I crawl toward her.

I make it within a foot and collapse, unable to draw a breath. Wheezing, I reach for her, and she blinks. Slowly and for a second, I see her true face.

"It's okay. Don't ever blame yourself." I try to tell her everything I can before it's too late. "I love you, Lali. Thank…" I can't finish as a fit of coughing takes my voice and my breath. Blood splatters over those silver wings.

I'm thankful for the moments of peace and joy she brought me and grateful I didn't fail my last task.

I awoke her powers, and they are beautiful destruction.

CHAPTER 19

CITLALI

I am eternal death.

No mercy.

I can take you quietly, peacefully letting you drift away, or I can slaughter you in a haze of pain.

None can stop the Reaper.

"...you for making me feel worthy." The words cut through the haze of anger and fear, and I hear a sound I've heard often in the emergency room. A final breath.

"No!" I blink and try to focus around the flames dancing in my vision.

When I finally do, I see him. Arkyn. He's lying on the floor, blood still running from his mouth and eyes. No. No. No.

I feel myself rocking back and forth. I don't know when I fell to my knees but I'm here, his blood on my skin and the revolting wings. I open my mouth and shriek like a banshee.

I hope someone hears my cry.

Sitara appears, and I cringe at her gasp. "I didn't mean to." Looking up, I feel tears start to pour from my eyes. "I tried to help him. I thought I was, and then he said something about Heaven and I got scared." She comes and kneels at my side, reaching for him.

"He's gone." She shakes her head. "There's nothing I can do."

A sob breaks from my throat. "Please."

She shakes her head. "I can't, but maybe you can. Raphael was the Bringer of Life and Death. The second, very few knew about or witnessed. You are his descendant. Only you might have the power to bring Arkyn back to us."

A sound draws my eyes toward the door. They all stand gathered, watching. Judging. Fearful.

Of me. They are terrified of me now. I shake my head. "I didn't mean to." My breath speeds up as I get more upset.

Lillian and Charlie both shake off the hands of their mates and rush forward.

"We know," Lillian murmurs, her hand gripping one of mine.

"I almost burnt Dagen to ash. I really understand." Charlie grabs the other.

"Arkyn said you connected with him when he was hurt, when he had…" She doesn't say the rest. She doesn't say when he had decided to die. She doesn't need to. I wonder if that's why I was able to reach him. "Try again."

Lucifer appears, and I jerk back. He holds up his hands, and I feel like such a bitch when I see the hurt in his eyes. I can hear Charlie grinding her molars and I glance at Lillian. I realize in that instant how protective these women are of him. Satan.

"You have to try to find him in the darkness, Citlali." His tone is imploring. Does Lucifer beg?

I look up into his eyes and wonder for a moment if this version is the true Lucifer. Did my fear of a creature I didn't even truly believe in kill Arkyn?

"Connect, Citlali. You don't have much time." Sitara's words jerk me from my thoughts.

I pray to a God I've never worshipped. Please help me. Please don't let me fail.

Opening my mind, I close my eyes and block everything out, searching for the thread that links us. As I search, I hear Charlie start to tap out a beat while she hums something beautiful. The beat reminds me of those at powwows, which reminds me of Arkyn. Thank you, Charlie.

I take a deep breath, holding it before letting it out slowly. Arkyn.

Pain. Sadness. Love.

The emotions hit me like a train.

Arkyn.

"I feel him. So much despair. So much pain." I choke on my shame. "I did this." Hands tighten on mine.

"Raphael was a healer, Citlali. You are a healer. Focus on that." Sitara's words cut through my self-pity, my disgrace.

I think of when he had stared at my wings in wonder and I had wrapped them around us.

"Holy shit."

"Oh my God, it's beautiful."

"I can feel it."

I ignore them all.

"Lillian, your scar." The uncertainty in the man's words forces my eyes open and to my left.

The red, raised scar I had noticed when first meeting her is smoother. Healed. The fingers of her free hand come to her face and tears form in her eyes.

"Thank you." The one called Torryn's voice is thick with emotion, and I look over at him but he only has eyes for her.

"Focus on Arkyn." Sitara is stern but I recognize her intention.

Closing my eyes once more, I try to send that power

through the connection I have with his soul or essence, whatever.

I have no idea how to do this. The thought plays over and over in my mind.

"You are doing it." Lucifer's breath whispers over my face as he leans near. I open my eyes and focus on his. This close, I'm amazed at them. There, swirling in their depths, is the cosmos. Breathtaking. I'm so focused on him, I connect, my power reaching for the part of him so broken by his past. By his Father. "No, Lali." He shakes his head. "Not me. Arkyn. Bring him back."

He shoves me out, breaking the connection. I consider how he did it, how he forced me out.

Pulling my hands free, I place them on Arkyn in the spots I would place a defibrillator in the hospital. Magic, power, electricity, it's all the same. I stare at my hands. Time to bring him back to me.

Deep cleansing breath, in then out, repeat. I let the warmth of the power build in me. I shape it, feeling my wings stretch up and curve around all five of us there on the floor. I hear Charlie sigh and I wonder what they see.

One more deep breath and then I send it like a bolt of lightning down through me.

"Arkyn!" I scream his name at the same time and hear glass shatter.

"Fucking hell," one of the men shouts.

I draw more power, sending it streaking down into Arkyn's body, sending it searching for his soul.

I yell his name again, making my voice as commanding as possible.

I feel his awareness in my mind the same moment I feel him draw a breath. I collapse over him sobbing.

I am sweet salvation.

Eternal mercy.
I can raise you up from the darkness.
None can stop the Bringer of Life.

CHAPTER 20

ARKYN

I am ripped from the darkness, from the never-ending pain, and from the eternal nothing.

She drags me from it. Her and her will alone brings me back.

Her scream shatters the darkness.

I can do nothing but obey.

The weight of her collapses on me. I struggle to lift my arms, to pull her close.

"You did it, Citlali," Luc murmurs from somewhere near.

"We need to leave here. Theon will have felt that explosion of power." Sitara sounds farther away.

"So will have Seraphina." Lillian is at my side.

"Hold on to him, Citlali." Luc's power courses through us, but I can still hear her crying in my mind.

'I killed you. I killed you,' she sobs over and over.

'No. Not you. The power. I felt you healing me before. I didn't understand. You didn't understand the duality of it. You healed me, you were healing me. You just got scared.'

'What happens next time I get scared? I could have killed them all.'

'But you didn't.'

Luc brings us to the temple. I open my eyes in a room I hadn't seen before. Lali is holding me tightly, and wrapping my arms around her, I squeeze her just as tight.

"You saved me," I whisper in her ear as I pull her up into my lap.

"From myself." I smile against her hair.

"Maybe. But you still saved me." Placing my finger under her chin, I turn her face up to meet my eyes, then use it to wipe away her tears.

She opens her mouth to argue with me, but I cover her lips with my own, kissing her deeply, exploring the heat, and pouring myself into her. I kiss her until we are both gasping for breath, and Luc clears his throat.

"I love you," she whispers against my lips, then moves farther away and says louder, "I will spend eternity making this up to you and the others."

"None of the others blame you for any of this. Nor does Arkyn." Luc's tone brooks no argument.

She swivels on my lap, turning to face him. Her power flares a little, but he shakes his head.

"I don't want to be healed, Citlali." Opening her mouth, she draws a breath to argue with the King of Hell, but something like an explosion rocks the temple and us. We all jump to our feet and race into the large main room of the temple.

"They have found us," Sitara shouts from the opening of the altar room. She stands with her arms raised, power visibly flowing from her hands. "I can buy us some time but not much. Theon has been closing in since he found Citlali. I tried to hide the temple, but it's too late."

Luc calls out to the others, his power breaching the wards she has erected just as she flies backwards. She hits the stone altar, and we hear her back break. She makes no noise as she slides to the ground. Even injured, maybe dying, she fights to hold the ward, but I can see Theon and Seraphina just beyond the opening to the tunnel now.

Lali races to her, but she shakes her head. "Don't let them see your power. He will take you at all cost, exploit you and it for eternity. You cannot let him." Lali shakes her head in denial. "Promise me."

She doesn't have time to respond as the wards drop.

The Fallen pour in, more than I've seen together. Ever. More than I knew even existed.

"Surprised, Morning Star?" Seraphina calls out from the opening where she, Theon, and the original Fallen stand waiting until we are overpowered. "Our ranks have grown exponentially since we first fell and even more since the girl showed them what they were missing."

He fights the first to reach him. I watch as he tries even now not to hurt them, to not kill them as they try to kill him.

They swarm him, completely ignoring me until I roar.

"What's little Arkyn going to do?" Her voice cuts through me like hot iron. Celine. "Nothing. Just like before. I've always wondered why Lucifer would bother to bring such a weak being back."

Laughter fills the cavernous room, and I feel myself locking down. Failure. Loser. Weak.

A scream drowns out the laughter, propelling me into motion, but I slide to a stop when I find them among the bodies.

Celine has Lali by the throat, dragging her toward the opening to Theon.

"Aren't you going to save her, Arky?" She smirks. "Save her like you did Uriel?" Laughter.

She looks at Lali, moving her mouth close to her ear. "Do you know how pathetically he died in Heaven? Did he tell you how easily I killed him?" She laughs as Citlali remains silent. "I didn't think so."

She drags her closer to Theon, who is smiling.

"Just bring the girl here, Celine." Theon looks beyond the two women and focuses on his sister. "If Sitara risked everything for her, she's special, so bring her to me."

"Didn't you already have her?" She snarls over her shoulder at him.

"I SAID BRING HER TO ME," he roars, and the temple vibrates from the force of it. Dust drifts down from the stone blocks, centuries old, a mixture of ash and other things burnt in the temple for hundreds of years. Celine's eyes narrow but she doesn't dare respond.

They come to a stop between Seraphina and Theon.

"You can use your powers to free yourself." Theon leans close to Lali, but his eyes are locked on Sitara.

"I don't need to; Arkyn will save me, no matter what you do or where you take me." My gaze bounces to hers.

Cackling laughter fills the air. Celine is such a fucking bitch. Luc is still fighting the others, slowly making his way through the masses. Knocking a group back, he circles away from them, moving around until he's in front of Sitara. Protecting her.

"Remember what I told you." I'm frozen, a cold sweat covering my body. "She believes the same."

I look back at the woman who has chosen me. She smiles just as they disappear. Animals howl and call throughout the jungle surrounding us as some of the Fallen stop in their tracks. Ice falls from above as heat scalds our feet.

My brothers have arrived.

CHAPTER 21

Theon has taken the three of us far away.

I'm alone in a room. Straining, I listen for them but hear nothing so I tiptoe across the polished wood floor to the door and lay my ear against it.

Silence.

Wrapping my hand around the cut crystal knob, I turn it a millimeter at a time. I wait to hear it squeak loudly, the sound echoing through the building like in every horror movie I've ever seen.

Looking down, I'm happy that my feet are bare. At least I won't be another cliché, falling in my heels while the murderer stalks me. The knob finally stops turning, no noise, and I turn my head, glancing at the hinges.

They appear almost new so maybe I can get out of this room without making any noise. It opens easily, and I slide out.

I might believe that Arkyn will find and save me but I'm going to give him every advantage I can. The hallway is empty, and I can see the outside through an open door.

Nerves skitter through me. Either this is a trap, or they

have dumped me so far from anything that it doesn't matter if I get out of the house. No better time to test my theories. I race at the open door and sail through it. A city, not mine, is just beyond a pristine yard.

My brain screams at me to stop, but I don't. I run headlong at the ornate gate under the vine-covered arch.

Magic throws me backwards. I land back near the door, twenty-five feet from the gate. I hear the bones break as they make contact with the stone steps I hadn't even noticed as I raced towards freedom.

Theon appears, towering over me, blocking the sun.

"Welcome to Avalon." He smiles. "I'm afraid you've broken your back. Will it heal, do you think?"

I don't answer as I wiggle my toes. They move slightly, thank God. I didn't manage to sever my spinal cord.

"You could use your new powers to call out to Sitara, and she could fix you right up." He smiles bigger.

I wonder if maybe I had a little help hitting the steps as hard as I did. Tears run out the corners of my eyes from the pain radiating down my arms and legs.

"You could call to Arkyn." The one called Celine steps to my side and leans over, her face inches from mine. "Not that he could or would do anything. You picked yourself a real winner."

I don't say anything, just watch her. "I hope he does come though. I think watching me kill you will be the best torture I have ever done to him."

I frown at her words.

"Wondering what else I've done?" She sounds too gleeful, and I know I don't want to know any of it. She looks over at Theon. "Should we move her or just let her lie out here and enjoy the city, enjoy the sinners?" I let my eyes travel over the buildings across the way. They don't reek of sin, so I'm not sure what I would be enjoying.

When I glance back up at them, he's looking at me. "I don't pick the cities. I couldn't care less about what you stupid, useless humans do, sins or not. But Seraphina likes to visit a certain group of places, time after time." He shrugs and looks at Celine. "I'll move her to the lounger." She frowns, but there in the yard sits a lounger that wasn't there a moment ago. She rolls her eyes as magic lifts me. I scream out in pain and I pray he doesn't sever the cord now. He draws very close as she stands watching him. "They like to believe the propaganda about sins so they don't have to admit they are just killers." His voice is low. "Killers are all they are. They just happen to be packaged in gorgeous wrappers."

His eyes skate over Celine, and I see hunger. I throw up in my mouth a little. The magic tightens on my back, and I cry out.

"We all have hungers," he growls as he lowers me to the chair. "Welcome to Amsterdam."

Another chair manifests across from me, and he lowers himself into it. Celine starts our direction, her hips rolling as she looks at him like she's about to devour him, not in a good way, like she might literally devour him. He smiles at her, raising an eyebrow, and I feel like I'm caught in some creepy porn.

I'm tempted to try to use my powers to heal myself just so I can get away from them. Another chair appears, and she practically melts into it.

She makes a noise before dragging her eyes to me. "So, where was I? Oh, that's right—the ways I tortured Arkyn since we both arrived here. It was really quite brilliant. We knew the 'Princes'..." She rolls her eyes at the title, "didn't remember their heavenly tasks, but it didn't take me long to figure out that Arkyn was still drawn to the natives." She grins as the pieces begin to click into place. "Like Eden did with Dagen, I drove them to extinction, or at least towards it."

I let my eyelids fall closed as tears spring to my eyes. So many tribes, cultures, and people lost. My people.

"I did it slowly. Every time he showed up, I would make sure they were destroyed. I liked the massacres, like Wounded Knee, the most."

"You are the demon," I spit through clenched teeth.

"How dare you? Those heathens didn't even worship the true God," she roars as she leaps to her feet, fists clenched.

"Which was your Archangel?" I ask quietly, watching her.

"Mine? He was never mine." She growls. "I was never his!" Her anger rolls through the air. I raise a brow waiting. "Uriel." It sounds like a curse on her tongue, and then she draws a deep breath, calming herself. Her hand comes up, smoothing her hair. "I gutted him. Arkyn raced into my home and stood frozen, staring at the mighty Uriel bleeding out, and did nothing. He didn't even fight back when I killed him. Pathetic." She laughs as she remembers. "Do you know what he said as I drove my sword through him?"

I shake my head, feeling more tears stream down my face.

"He looked at me with those sad pathetic eyes and said 'You can still be forgiven by Him. I forgive you.' He forgave me as I killed him. What a fucking loser."

She walks away, going in the house, stopping in the doorway to beckon Theon.

He looks at me as he stands. "She's so much fun when she's this angry." He leans down and whispers 'thank you' in my ear.

Revulsion rushes through me.

They leave me laying on the lounger, pain ripping through me. I can feel my powers trying to flare to life but I keep them and the wings shoved down inside me. Sitara may have omitted some things she should have told me but she has never lied. Her warning was rushed and dangerous, so I will heed it.

I reach out to him but I'm not sure if it will make it past whatever magic is surrounding this place. Avalon. It's not what I have ever imagined. A story for Lillian if I make it out of here, since she said she had been held with Seraphina. She must have lived within it.

'Please hurry, Arkyn.'

Pain lances through me as I'm hit with more magic. I've reached my limit and I can feel consciousness slipping away as internal bleeding begins to fill my cavities.

'Amsterdam.'

Darkness engulfs me just as I hear footsteps, stilettos clicking on stones.

"Is she dead?" It is the other one's voice, Seraphina. I wish I could say 'no but probably soon if you just wait, you miserable puta.'

I smile in my mind and let myself drift away.

CHAPTER 22

ARKYN

The battle ended hours ago, and the temple has once again been home to sacrifice. Blood coats its walls and fills the intricate carved pattern on the floor.

Evander had truly been a demon. Not just killing but slaughtering those that dared cross his path.

Lucifer had disappeared right after Citlali to track her, taking Sitara with him and hoping she could find Theon. I'm standing here feeling useless as I patch the others up. That's me, putting a bandaid on your boo-boo.

My head whips up. I feel her. Pain rockets through me, and my demon breaks free, my wings snap out, and everyone freezes. Staring at me.

"What the fuck?" Dagen rushes towards me from where he was leaning against the altar. I step back as he draws close, hand outstretched. The problem is I didn't see Torryn coming from the other direction.

"Well, look who is all special and shit." I cringe as fingers slide over one of the long primary feathers.

I jerk, spinning away, and Zeph steps in front of me,

blocking them. I wish I could see his face because whatever is on it stops them both in their tracks.

"We were just kidding, Arkyn." Dagen's eyes are filled with remorse. "Do you know why they aren't midnight like ours?"

No way I'm saying 'because Luc said I'm special.' I shrug instead, but Torryn's eyes narrow.

Lillian and Charlie's mouths form perfect circles when they step into the room.

"So pretty," they say in unison, and their men frown. I grin.

"Lali's are silver and sparkle like diamonds," I murmur, and the women oooh over my words. The men frown more. "Lali." I shake my head, remembering what started all this. "I felt her, Zeph." He turns and nods.

"I bet they are like that because of your power." I turn and stare at Lillian. "Lightning. Silver until it hits something then boom. Black."

"You are so damn smart, sweetheart." Torryn wraps his arms around her.

"Citlali is hurt. Bad." Everyone stops, freezes, ready to go to war for me. "I connected with her for just a second, and the pain..." I lock my eyes on Zeph. "We have to get to her."

"Where?" Why he asks, I don't know. I can feel him digging through my brain.

"Amsterdam. That's all I know." I look at them all.

"Luc!" Lillian yells, but it's her power flowing out across the damn universe that he will hear.

He appears instantly, that baby girl in his arms. His eyes are wild. "Damn it, Lillian, don't do that. I was afraid another battle had broken out, that they had returned with more Fallen."

"So you brought the baby?" Charlie smirks. His face locks down, hiding his emotions.

"What do you want?" It's a thunderous growl, but the tiny hand that comes up and grabs at his full lower lip ruins the effect.

Some turn away to hide their laughter. I smile at it, and Torryn barks out a laugh.

"I need to get to Amsterdam. Now." I step around Zeph. Our leader sighs and hands Zeph the child. She smiles almost as dreamily at him as she does Luc, and I wonder if maybe he hasn't been babysitting.

"I'll take you, and the others can take the jet or use their own damn wings. Someone message Evander. Tell him to get one of Demon Bayou's employees to take care of the houses and your things." His hand clamps around my arm, and we break apart into nothing as he moves us around the world.

Moments or maybe seconds later, we are standing on a darkening street in Amsterdam, a canal to my left and people milling about. I turn slowly, focusing on her, trying to connect.

Nothing.

Now I understand Dagen's sense of helplessness when Charlie disappeared before our eyes.

Hours turn to days as I search. Sitara can't find Citlali; we believe Theon has found a new way to cloak her. Caliel can't find Avalon; his beacon died with Grace.

This is my sixth day and night searching the city, a city that has been plagued with freak storms since my arrival. My power's barely, okay, not really under my control. Lightning lights up the night again.

News stations have been constantly reporting on the freak lightning storms and not just local ones. Evander's ringtone fills the moment of silence as Zeph answers his phone quickly. He is my watch dog, making sure that I don't do something stupid like burn the city to the ground or fuck up in some other massive way.

He, of course, doesn't say that's what he's doing, but we both know what it is. Babysitter.

"I've told you, he's fine," he growls, and I face away, letting the wind blow my hair. It's loose, the way she left it, except the war braids at my temples, and the beads and trinkets attached to those make sounds that remind me of the wind chimes that hang from the four corners of my home. I focus on those sounds, pulling my powers back under control. "It's not as if you haven't been upset lately, so how about you cut him some slack."

Holy shit, the two words are drawn out into about sixteen syllables in my head. I look over my shoulder at my friend, at my brother, and see him for exactly what he is, maybe for the first time. Badass. I also understand and believe he truly is my friend. He punches the screen so hard on his phone I'm sure I hear it crack before he shoves it in his pocket.

His eyes are glowing a bright icy blue when they lock onto mine. "I've always had your back, brother, even before." He blinks and they go back to their normal dark blue with pale flecks through them. They remind me of a snow storm, like those in the north where he has always been more comfortable. "My powers didn't come from the demon. He only amplified what had already been there."

It is the night for me to stand around like an idiot with a shocked look on my face, I guess. The night sky calms as I focus on his revelation though.

"I didn't realize it until Luc released my memories but oh yes, I've always been able to see the true nature of people in their minds."

I, for one instant, think of how he could have stopped all of this. "People, not angels. That's how He amplified them. I do wish I could have known her plans, all of those *sukas* would have died well before they could have done any of this."

Anger radiates off of him, and I can see the warrior he tries to keep so well hidden.

Aren't we the pathetic pair?

CHAPTER 23

CITLALI

*L*ightning crashes, the song, plays through my head as I wish for death.

Wish for it because my powers won't let me die, but something either done by Theon, the others, or maybe this fucking house is also keeping them from healing me.

I've tried since the second day of laying on this Godforsaken lounger. I've tried to use them and I've tried to not, but neither works. Instead, I'm floating in a sea of pain and stench.

Bed sores have formed all along the underside of my body. After years of working in the jungle, I know the scent of dying flesh. I'm positive the cushion is soaked with not just my body fluids but also other worse things.

I only know the passing of the days because of the movement of the sun and the woman.

I noticed her on the first day. I noticed her because unlike every other person that walked by or paused with a map outside the wrought iron fence, she noticed me.

Whatever hides Avalon from the world, whatever makes it seem so unassuming, doesn't work on the woman. She has a routine, one that now includes coming near the corner of the fences. She never makes direct eye contact but she watches me, she watches the house. She stays somewhere near, and I've seen her on a rooftop down the block.

I let my eyes travel around the yard after I notice her movement coming up the street. Just like every moment since they left me here, I'm alone. More lightning crashes around the city. Arkyn.

She pauses at the brick corner pillars, like she has every day, leaning against it with the book open in her hands. Her eyes are scanning the grounds of Avalon, though they light on me only for seconds, narrowing, and I wonder if she is checking for signs of life.

Today is the day for me to take a chance.

I look around again, listening for signs of other life. Nothing.

"I don't know how you can see me. I know you understand this place is different. I know you understand there is more in this world than we can see." I pause, wishing I had been like her, aware of the more. "I need you to help me. I know you don't have any reason to but I'm begging you to." A sound catches my attention. Stilettos on tile, fucking angels, worst Goddamn timing. I lock my eyes on her, no time to waste on deception. "Demon Bayou Rum, call them and tell Arkyn where to find this place." I feel Theon even without seeing him. "Please."

She spins away just as the door opens, disappearing into the shadows the way she's done every day. They don't even stop or, hell, pause as they make their way down the walkway and out the gate.

Off to murder, I'm sure.

I hope they run into Arkyn and his brothers. My luck, they would kill them before they found out where I was, the demons that is.

I scan the rooftops, looking for the woman. I can't see her but that doesn't mean she isn't there. I kind of hope she isn't. I hope those damned demons have an office in this fucking town and the mystery woman is racing toward it as I lay here literally rotting.

I try again to reach out for Arkyn or any of them and once again scream out at the pain that ricochets through my brain.

Darkness sweeps through me. It is no slow fade to black, and I gladly let it take me away from everything, even as the brilliant flash of Arkyn's power lights up the sky.

There she is, outlined against the darkened sky. When did it get dark? How long was I out?

Before I can answer either of those questions, it turns into Hell on Earth outside the iron gate. My eyes are still locked on the woman, and I don't fail to see her head nod just once before she disappears.

CHAPTER 24

ARKYN

*T*hose of us with wings drop from the sky, death and retribution from above.

Torryn and Charlie bring Hellfire and heat with them. Dagen keeps the locals from being incinerated by bringing ice and water. We could use Evander, but he has been unpredictable to say the least. Luc has placed him back in New Orleans for now.

I haven't missed the strange whispered conversations between Dagen and Lillian; something very strange is going on, but no one is talking to me. Zeph is suspicious also. He's been flexing his powers, pushing at their mental blocks. His fault, for he taught us all how to keep him out. I just never bother; everyone knows my shame.

But those people got secrets. If anyone can get them out, it's Zeph. I've heard stories of him in Heaven. He was The Interrogator, the one who was sent to find out who had started the war. Luc gave him access to all of those that ended up in his domain. Zeph questioned every angel that died in the war. Luc pulled them from darkness and gave them to Zeph before sending them back to the nothing.

I can't imagine and I don't want to. Theon, Seraphina, and Celine have been joined by their newest recruits.

"Did you tell them they are cannon fodder?" Zeph calls out.

The newbies glance around, and I can smell the apprehension on the air. Get them, Zeph. I wonder if they feel his power drifting over them, through them.

He stokes their fears while Charlie and Torryn show them what their future will hold. Newbs. Too easy.

It is worrisome how many new recruits they have. In all the years since this stupid war started, all the time I've, we've, been hunting these fucking bitches, I've never seen this many at the same time. Sure, there's always been those that have grown hungry for the things they feel they are missing out on.

I can't blame them, especially now that I've gotten my memories back. Heaven is as bland as unflavored oatmeal. I wouldn't return for anything; give me Hell any day.

I let them deal with the new guys and focus on the ward around Avalon. Theon has done something to it. Even Sitara is unable to move through it. Dark magic is woven through it now. I can tell when the lightning hits it. I can see the blackened veins running throughout, like a plague, like a parasite feasting on blood.

I can see her, see my girl just in the yard, forgotten like some piece of trash. A figure moves between us, and I drag my eyes up the body. Celine. Literally the bane of my entire existence.

"Hello, Arky." She grins and waggles her fingers at me. "Here to fight?"

I don't respond.

"Didn't end well last time. You remember, right?" Her eyebrows raise as she waits. "I do." She glances over her shoulder at Lali. "I killed you. I cut you from stem to stern."

My molars grind together as I fight to keep my face blank. Her finger moves slowly from her crotch up the midline of her body, stopping just below her collarbone. There it slides under a gold chain I hadn't noticed before. Pulling it out, she grins bigger as I glance down at what is now hanging from that finger. I blink slowly as I try to understand what it is I'm looking at.

Zeph growls as he moves to my side, "You bitch, you fucking bitch."

I look over at him then back at the necklace, finally my brain makes sense of it.

"Now you got it." She giggles. "I took it after you were dead. Destroyed it so everyone would know you were spineless but I kept a couple had them gilded in gold and keep them close to my heart. They bring me great joy, Arky. Memories of a great day."

I watch as her fingers slide over the set of four of my smallest vertebrae.

My wings flare out and up, Lillian's eyes widen, and I glance back at them. They have changed. Even more different than before, now blackened forks of electricity are patterned through them. A belly-burning rage has broken free in me and it is fueling my powers.

'I love you. They are so beautiful.' Citlali's voice whispers through my mind. *'Make it rain, baby.'*

I let my hands float out away from my body and reach with my power, pulling electricity from the city's grid. I let it flow through me and then hit the barrier with everything I had in me. Two thousand years of every shitty thought I've ever had about myself channels into my power, releasing something new.

"Finally." Luc's voice echoes through the night.

I look at him through silver, my eyes having changed with my wings.

"Finally, what?" Torryn looks back and forth between us.

"Awe, it's a good thing you're so damn sexy, babe." Lillian shakes her head at him. He frowns at her, and Zeph chuckles. "He's glad Arkyn finally believes in himself, sweetheart."

"Oh. Well then, yeah, about Goddamn time." He turns back to the barrier and sends a wave of heat, one hot enough to melt the iron of the fence. "Keep it up, White Lightning. You're getting through."

I swear to Satan, he's like a big dumb lovable puppy but he's right. I can feel the power of the barrier wavering. I reach deeper, imagining that spine she said I didn't have, and I straighten it, letting the energy course through it.

Locking my gaze on Lali, I draw in a breath then release it slowly.

Time to save my avenging Angel of Death.

Focusing my strength like a laser, I just have to break one thread in the weave, one tiny string, and it all unravels. Sitara steps up to my shoulder, and I feel the delicate touch of her magic join mine. It moves over mine like a tendril of a vine. I can almost see it as it waits patiently at the edge of Avalon's protection.

"You've perverted this place that once protected us." Her voice is filled with sadness as she stares at her brother.

"YOU caused this. You," he spits as he yells at her. "You could have come with me."

"Are you fucking kidding me?" Torryn barks out a laugh. "All this because you've got some separation anxiety. Poor baby-waby, his little sissy didn't pick him for her team." The giant, tattooed beast pokes out his bottom lip and makes a sound like a small child.

Theon roars from the other side. I watch Celine and Seraphina as they feel their first hint of fear. Worry. Uncertainty.

I smile at them, pushing harder.

I will do this. I will break them. It will be me who opens the Gates of Hell to them. I will.

We all feel the barrier shudder. The tension sky rockets as we all prepare to go to war. Then something amazing happens. Avalon chooses sides.

It chooses us.

Avalon disappears.

Shock shines in the Fallen's eyes and it brings me joy. I let my power fall away. My eyes lock on her.

Citlali. The Angel of Death. My angel of dark destruction. She rises like a specter. Her bones shining through her all too thin skin, she looks on the verge of death herself. She's so fucking beautiful.

"Isn't my girl beautiful?" I glance around. "Whatever, assholes, she's gorgeous.

"Thank you, baby." She smiles, and I have to admit the blood stain on her teeth leaves a little to be desired.

Wings burst from her back, silver satin feathers literally glowing from within as her power sweeps out of her. First her body heals before our very eyes. I didn't think it was possible but she's even more amazing. Heavenly.

She slowly rotates as she floats off the ground, her eyes locking on Seraphina and Celine. Seraphina disappears, leaving Celine, who tries to flee when she realizes her fearless leader has abandoned her. My girl has other plans for her though.

Death grips her tight, holding her in this place where it was tortured.

Her voice is dark and layered with venom when she speaks. "I have it in my power to send you to the darkness with a snap of my finger." A hand floats up and fingers are poised to do just that but it doesn't. "I can be merciful or I can do to you what you did to Arkyn."

Those delicate, sensitive fingers point at the necklace still clutched in Celine's hand. It disappears and reappears in Lali's palm. She strokes over the pieces of my spine lovingly before slipping the necklace over her head.

"A symbol of your strength. Keeping you close to my heart. Always." Her voice sounds so strange, a bit creepy, but I can hear nothing but love, can see nothing but pride in her midnight eyes. She smiles eerily before looking back at Celine. "How long have I been here?"

I glance at Zeph, who grimaces as his head tilts, leaving it up to me.

"Seven days." I hate admitting that. "I've searched seven days since you contacted me."

She nods once.

"Not the snap of a finger then." Death shines bright and retribution rings in her voice.

We all stand frozen as she rises higher in the air, taking Celine with her. Higher and higher until they are small in the sky. Citlali draws the angel to her, speaking to her. Those of us with supernatural hearing can just hear the sound of it. Words are lost in the winds.

Lillian gasps and Charlie screams as they begin to fall.

Celine screams and fights, but Citlali holds her tight with hands and magic.

We all watch as she drives her into the ground. The sound of her spine breaking echoes around us. Fucking shattering.

Lali straightens and death stares at us all.

"Move her to the lounger."

Zeph starts forward to do as she says, but I reach out and stop him. I will help my angel.

Bending down, I whisper in Celine's ear, "Now who doesn't have a spine?"

She screams as I drag her to the lounger.

"Sitara, set a ward. It's time for us to go."

I turn around and there is Lali. Death has receded. I walk to her, pulling her into my arms.

"Except you, Zeph. I think you should stay around here. Watch the rooftops."

His eyes scan them as soon as the words leave her mouth.

Charlie steps close to him and leans in, her mouth close to his ear.

"I have heard an interesting beat in this town."

CHAPTER 25

CITLALI

*D*eath wants to claim more. Hundreds. Thousands. But Arkyn calls to me, the woman, the healer. I focus on that call and return to him, tucking the dark side of my power away.

I let the light side of the power surge forward.

It floats on the air through the city, healing those that are sick and broken before I can rein it in.

I glance around as those close to me make soft sighing sounds. Shit. They all look a little more—more healthy, more youthful, more everything.

"Sorry," I mumble against Arkyn's chest.

"Don't apologize, sweetheart." He rubs his hands over my back.

Searching for the break, I can tell, but it's healed, like it never happened. I turn my head and look at Celine. Maybe it's like it didn't happen but it most certainly did.

"Take me away, Arkyn." Looking at the faces that surround us, I continue, "Leave her. Seven days and she will wither and die. The darkness will take her, and even you,

Lucifer, will not be able to pull her free." I feel Death looking out at the King of Hell, who only nods.

"Why would I wish to, Citlali?" His voice is beautiful and melodic.

If he had been gorgeous before, now he is something otherworldly. I feel mesmerized by his eyes, the cosmos glowing in them.

Dragging my gaze away from him, I look at the woman that has been my mother for almost my entire life. She looks like Sitara but different, and I wonder if this is her true form. I doubt it, somehow.

"Where would you like to go, my love?" Arkyn whispers in my ear.

"Anywhere. I would go anywhere with you."

He smiles at my words, at the truth he can hear in them. I let my fingers travel over the wings curved against his shoulders; they remind me of the velvet I like to wrap around me when I sleep.

"Maybe we should all stay here in the city. Just in case," Dagen suggests as he leads Charlie away, fingers intertwined, heated looks shared between them. "We have the office building with the penthouse above it."

Lillian and Torryn nod and start to follow them.

"I need to check on the baby." Luc's voice is low as he fades away.

"Are you keeping her?" Lillian stops and turns back to look at him.

I have no idea what baby they are speaking about, but it is curious. Lucifer with a baby. Sitara is watching him closely, her interest piqued as well.

"I don't know, Lillian. She seems to calm the demon."

I frown, as do the others, except Lillian and Dagen. Those two glance at each other.

A noise hums in Arkyn's chest, and Zeph's eyes narrow. Luc disappears before anyone can say anything.

"Secrets can destroy the greatest bonds." I look at those that clearly know the secret. "Or they can make them stronger, if shared with those that can be trusted."

I watch as Arkyn and his brothers study each other. Brothers in every way but blood.

Lillian sighs, "Let's all go to the penthouse. I have something to tell you. All."

I look up at Arkyn and see that worry creases his forehead, clouds his eyes. Not for himself but for those he cares about, for Luc. I know the last because I see his eyes dart to the spot Lucifer vacated moments ago.

I'm beginning to understand each of these men, and the women that are joining them, myself included, worry a great deal for the King of Hell.

It takes us all mere moments to travel across town to the city center. There, rising up from the skyline, is the Demon Bayou Rum company offices, with the skull and live oak emblem lit up in blue neon.

The men stroll in, a simple nod given to the security at the desk, and we're heading straight to the elevators.

Once inside, Zeph steps to the panel and types in six-six-six enter.

"Oh my God, really?" Charlie laughs, and Lillian and I join in.

Zeph shrugs, Torryn grins, and Arkyn and Dagen shake their heads.

"It's easy to remember." Zeph actually gets the words out with a straight face.

I realize it's because he isn't kidding, at all.

"Zeph doesn't joke," Arkyn whispers in my ear. "Do you?"

The man, or demon, in question shakes his head. "These idiots forgot every code I set until I decided to use this one."

"Zeph is the head of all our security, here on Earth and in Hell," Torryn offers, and the pride in his voice is so sweet. I look back and up at Arkyn as the elevator begins to rise.

"Public relations," he mumbles at my unasked question.

"Arkyn is the face of Demon Bayou." Dagen holds out his phone, and I see a photo is pulled up.

"For the love of God, Dagen, are you fucking kidding me?" He pushes the phone away but not before I see it, see him.

High hat on his head with feathers sticking out, a white wife beater shirt, jeans slung low on his slim hips, and make-up on his face to make him look like a demon voodoo priest.

Fucking sexy as hell.

I blink as his voice penetrates the lust clouding my brain. "That's all I was good at being, the face."

"What?" Dagen, Torryn, and Zeph all spin to stare at Arkyn, all three of their voices angry at his self-deprecating words.

The elevator slides open, and we all shuffle out, awkwardness thick around us all.

"Luc chose you because of the outreach component of the job. You care more about humans than any of us. You are the least volatile of us all. You are the most redeemable of us all."

I watch his face as his brothers talk about him; I see the discomfort the words bring him. My sweet, damaged man.

"You have so much power within you, Arkyn. We saw it today—that was you, not someone else. It came from you; it has always been there just waiting for you to tap into it. To find it, to unleash it."

"Celine did so much damage that day in Heaven, not just killing you but somehow convincing you deep in your soul of your unworthiness, so much so that even without your memories, it ate at you for hundreds and hundreds of years." Zeph paces away, frustration bleeding from his very pores.

"Come on, Arkyn." I grab his hand and pull him toward the couch. I sit and settle myself, dragging him down with me. "So…"

I remind them of why we all came here. The secret. I just joined this fight; I refuse to let it start to fall apart now because people are hiding things.

The others move around, finding places to sit. Zeph is at a bar at the side of the room. He turns after pouring a large glass of some clear liquid; I'm one hundred percent it isn't rum or water.

He throws the entire amount down his throat. Damn. Okay, I don't know him well but I'd say Zeph has some idea of what this secret is and it isn't good.

Lillian and Dagen stand shoulder to shoulder. Torryn is frowning and Charlie has one brow raised. We all wait. Impatiently. Dagen glances down at the woman at his side and she shakes her head.

"I'm not telling them. He told you, brought you in on it." He uses his hand at the small of her back to push her slightly forward.

Her eyes narrow as she spins, and sword appearing in her hand, the point ends up resting against the slow beat of his heart in his neck. He doesn't move at all.

"Very funny, Princess." He uses his finger to push the blade away.

"I said I didn't want to tell them."

"Well, you told me, and now they know you told me." He sighs and his hand runs over his close-cropped hair. "We need help. You said yourself that the situation isn't getting better. A decision will be made soon, and I honestly don't want him to have to do it on his own."

Tears spring to her eyes. Torryn sits up straight, an angry noise coming from his throat. "Don't make her cry, asshole." A warning that Dagen shakes his head at.

"It's not his fault, babe." Lillian hugs Dagen from the side then steps away. She walks a couple steps and then stops, turning back to us. "Grace is alive."

I can tell from the looks on the others' faces that this is momentous. I have no idea who Grace is, but she's very important, that much is clear.

The silence is deafening, pushing in at us all.

Torryn shoves himself up. "Evander." One word but it is laced with so many emotions. "It's tearing him apart."

He levels them both with a look that makes me feel like I'm back with the nuns. Disappointment.

"Luc wouldn't let me tell anyone," Lillian starts but Torryn's face stops her. "Yes, well, Dagen was watching me so closely, and I just... I had to tell someone."

Dagen shakes his head.

"And you? What's your excuse?" Torryn stares at his friend.

"I haven't even seen the angel in question but from what I've heard..." he looks at Lillian hard, "it isn't good."

"She hasn't changed from her demon form. Luc can't figure out if she can't or if she refuses. She kills or destroys everything and only calms slightly when I visit." Lillian has tears running down her face by the time she finishes. "He's given her a few more weeks before he sends her back to the darkness."

Torryn wraps her in his arms, trying to soothe her all the while glaring at Dagen.

I lean close to Arkyn. "Who's Grace?"

"That is a very long story. But the short version is that she is and always has been Evander's one true soulmate, created for him by the Lord and killed by Seraphina."

Shit. The word slips through my lips as I draw it out, which has around twenty syllables by the time I'm finished.

"But he said the baby…" I say it loud enough that they all turn and look at me.

"The baby." Lillian straightens a bit from where she had curled into Torryn.

"I told you she was special. That little angel has an amazing song that was meant for Luc." Charlie sounds giddy.

It's Zeph that I look at, study really. He is quiet, assessing, processing the information.

"We do not tell him," he says finally after several minutes. The others have been arguing about calling their boss. They fall silent when Zeph speaks, his Russian accent thicker than I've heard it before.

"It means he's angry." I glance to my left at Arkyn's face. He's smiling, and I frown. "This is going to be good."

We sit silent as the man lectures the others for at least an hour. Most I understand, but many times he fell into speaking Russian.

He stalks to the elevator, jabs the buttons, and then looks back locking his eyes on all of us.

"You will not destroy him once again."

We will all heed the threat we hear in his words.

CHAPTER 26

ARKYN

*D*estroyed.

I think of the destruction that Evander wrought in the temple. Luc had sent him back to New Orleans after. Or did he?

"Where's Boss at?" Torryn spins at my question.

"At headquarters," he responds but Lillian's face says it all.

"Lillian?" I hate to see the look of hurt that flares to life in Torryn's eyes.

"I'm sorry. I wanted to tell you. All of you. But Luc wanted to give him time to get control." She reaches for Torryn as she speaks. He remains stiff for a moment but then takes her hand. "He's in Hell. Locked in his room to keep him and others safe."

"Others?" Lali asks quietly.

Lillian sighs as she sits, letting her fingers slip from Torryn's hand. She seems as sad as she was when we first found her.

"He went back to New Orleans, but there were some issues. He couldn't stop." The last word is said so quietly that I almost didn't hear it.

"Stop?" I lean toward her.

"Killing." She looks up at my face, and I see now that tears are streaming down her face. "He killed so many before Luc realized."

Shock. Complete shock silences us all.

"It's not fair for him to put this on you. To force you to keep his secrets." Torryn wraps an arm around her shoulders but he looks at me, and I can see the anger simmering in his eyes. They flicker red.

"He didn't. He doesn't even know I know. I went to check on Grace and I could hear this roaring. It sounded insane, crazed like an animal caught in a trap, so…"

"You went to look." Torryn shakes his head.

"He didn't recognize me." She starts to shake, then the first sob breaks free.

"Fuck," I murmur locking eyes with my brother.

Evander's demon is the strongest of all of ours. He was the strongest of us in Heaven, now with the powers of both. Unlocked, he would be like no demon ever unleashed on the Earth.

The demon has control and it wants revenge for all that the angel has lost.

What he has lost is right down the hall, so to speak.

"Fuck." I can't help but say it again. Really there isn't any other word or sentiment that sums up the situation. "So, to sum up our current situation, we have a crazy Lumerian but we don't know exactly how powerful he is, but he's determined to kill us all because his sister didn't pick him. We have the Fallen, who seem to be on a recruiting drive. A boss that is locked in Hell because his demon is determined to kill any and everything. And last but not least, his soulmate is also locked in Hell because Luc dragged her, kicking and screaming, from the darkness, and if we even tried to put them together, their demons would destroy each other and God only knows what else."

"You forgot we still have to find the other descendants," Charlie offers, smiling at the look I give her.

"Are we going to tell Zeph?" Torryn shakes his head even as he asks the question.

"What good would it do?"

Sitara pushes off the wall, startling the others that had forgotten her presence.

"I must go."

Citlali stands and walks to her side, and I try to catch their whispered words as the others continue the heated debate on what we should do next.

Sitara simply fades away, and Lali is left staring out the window at the city.

"Everything okay?" Dagen glances at Lali before giving me a nod.

Lali's voice sounds distant. "A ward was set off around the temple."

"Could it be the locals?" I doubt Dagen really believes that himself.

"No, it's set for supernatural creatures." She still hasn't turned from the window. She's staring in the direction of where she was held.

Where Celine is lying, dying slowly at Lali's hand. I can see her face reflected in the glass; it is stamped with worry and anger.

Looking around, the faces in the room are a myriad of emotions.

"Come on, love, nothing to be done tonight, and I have missed you." I watch that glass and am rewarded with a slow smile before she turns. She walks straight to me and into my arms.

I nod at the others as I guide her away and down the long

hallway that skirts the outer wall. I've always loved this building; it had once been a grand hotel.

The sitting room we had just been in overlooks the glass-enclosed atrium. Employees covet the interior offices that have large glass walls looking into that atrium. Here on the top floor, it's the bedrooms that looks into it but here, the glass wall is mirrored for privacy.

I lead her down the hall until it makes a hard left, and then we keep going until it comes to another. Right past that turn is the door to the room I long ago claimed as mine. In the mornings, it is beautiful from this angle with the early sunlight.

Closing the door, I lean against it until she stops at the edge of the large bed, facing the glass.

"I need to hold you." I watch as she smiles that smile at me.

She doesn't move, just waits for me, and I don't make her wait long. I'm across the distance in a split second, pulling at her clothes, needing to touch her, to make sure she really is healed. Make sure she is really here.

Her hands are in my hair, pulling me closer, pressing her lips against mine. I suck her lower one into my mouth. She opens to me, and I taste the dark chocolate cinnamon that is uniquely her. Like the hot chocolate I used to get on the reservation. Thick and intoxicating, just like the woman.

My hands slide down over her waist to the curve of her hips. Fingers curve, digging in and pulling her against me. Here with her in private, I don't have any self-doubt. She sees me, and I see her. I can be whatever she wants, demanding alpha or submissive beta. I will be her everything.

Applying more force to the kiss and my hands, I wait to see which Arkyn she wants. The low moan is my answer.

Alpha it is.

One benefit of being supernatural and having lived for

thousands of years is having acquired enough wealth to not worry about small things...like clothes.

I release her hips and break the kiss, stepping back a step. She frowns. Raising my hand, I focus on my demon and watch her eyes widen as razor sharp claws slide from the ends of my fingers. She had dressed herself in jeans and a loose top when she was finally free and healed.

One long black claw slides down the seam of those jeans on each side as a slow smile curves her lips. They slice through the fabric easily, then I use those and the other claws to jerk the fabric from her. The strength of the jerk rips what wasn't cut.

A heated gasp escapes her, and I grin at her, knowing it looks feral when she bites at her lower lip.

She shivers as those claws glide gently over her skin, coming up and sliding under the lace of her panties. The satin and lace are no match for me. They flutter to the floor in seconds.

I stare at her as she stands before me, bare from the waist down. Moisture glistens on the dark hair hiding her core. Reaching for the hem of her shirt, she watches me closely, but I stop her with a shake of my head.

"Don't you want me undressed?" Her voice is breathy.

I shake my head and her pupils flare. I let the claws slide away as I wrap my hand around her neck, turning her body, guiding her with pressure along her pounding pulse until her ass is pressed back against me.

I kiss along the free side of her neck while sliding my finger up to her jaw. I turn her face back to me and take her mouth, forcing my way inside while my other hand moves around her waist and down until I find the moisture I had seen.

Her hips shift forward. Seeking. Needing.

One finger sinks into her, and her head drops back onto

my shoulder, breaking the kiss, but I forgive her as her hand comes up to grip the back of my head, directing my lips to her neck as she gasps in pleasure.

"So wet," I murmur against the vein in her neck as I feel my fangs lengthen.

"Need you."

Those words and the fact that I know they are true drive my own need, turning it primal.

Pumping my finger in and out of her as I lick over her neck, I fight the urge to bite her, to drink her down. My hand, still on her jaw, slides down to her neck once more and then I push her forward, bending her over. I let go as she complies. She is perfection as I pull my finger from her and step back.

I feast on the sight of her—legs straight, ass high, head on the bed with her arms stretched out. Perfection.

I hit my knees, and she jumps a little from the noise of it. She is bare and open to me, waiting, and my hands have a mind of their own as they reach out and grasp her ass, spreading her flesh even more. Another shudder works through her muscles and drops of moisture leak from her body.

I catch them and savor the taste of her. As soon as it hits my tongue, I feel my control slipping away. I reach down and open my pants, pulling myself free and running my hand over the hard, pulsing length of my dick even as I lean forward and take her into my mouth. I suck and bite as she makes mewling sounds and pushes back, wanting more. Needing more. I plunge my tongue in and pull it out, lapping at her heated flesh, all the while stroking myself.

"More, Arkyn," she demands as she shoves back against my face.

I growl in response and nip at her swollen bud, but she only moans louder and more juice flows from her body.

"Fuck, Lali." I barely get the words out before I turn my head slightly and bite, sinking my fangs into the vein that runs there just below the skin. I drink down the coppery fluid, drawing deeply on her as I shove two fingers into her heat. The flesh convulses around them as she screams.

It's my name. It is my undoing. I can wait no longer. I lick at the wounds and rise, positioning myself at her entrance even as I withdraw my fingers.

I press against her tight entrance, and she presses back even as she pushes up on one arm, back bowing up and hair cascading down. It is a sight I will never forget.

I grip her hips and hold her in place as I shove through the swollen folds of flesh until I'm buried deep. I pause there, wrapped in her velvet heat, trying to gain control, but she won't have it and rotates her hips slightly.

I pull back until I can see the glistening length of me poised to shove forward and I do. Over and over, long, hard, deep strokes until we both lose control, her pushing back against every hard pound forward, matching me stroke for stroke until we are both soaring closer and closer to the edge of our release.

I feel it begin like a fire burning up my legs just as her body clutches at mine.

I yell her name as I sink into her one last time, filling her with my release. I collapse over her, and she sinks completely to the mattress as her muscles milk at my twitching cock. We both work to catch our breath.

"I love you," I whisper the words against her neck. "You have saved me...from myself."

CHAPTER 27

CITLALI

I feel the darkness recede. Death returns to the darkness; it has been beating at me all night, lying in wait just below the surface, fighting for control.

I think he is the one saving me.

The Angel of Death scares me, because the power it offers is a temptation I'm afraid I can't deny. It whispers of the lives I could save, of the ones I could take. It shows me those near that deserve death, that have earned it.

Their deaths call to me, but he has quieted them. He calls to my healer side, the side that wants to save. Even now, held in his arms, my power reaches out and sends tendrils to those sick that are near.

"You can't heal everyone, Lali," he murmurs against my neck as he rolls to the side, pulling me against me as he does.

"I can't control it yet."

"I know, but death is a part of life. Death is just the next step. The start of another journey."

I like the sound of that. "Tell me about it."

"That could take awhile." He shifts again, moving off the

CHOSEN MAGIC

bed, and pulls me with him. "Let's shower, and then if you still want to hear, I'll tell you."

I let him lead me to the bathroom and join him after I pull my shirt off, dropping it to the floor. At first, I stand at the back of the shower that could hold many more people, watching as the water slides over his body. I study the tattoos. He isn't covered like the one called Torryn but he has a raven whose wings span his shoulders. It is realistic and yet has tribal symbols woven into and around it. A dedication to the people he has forever championed. My fingers reach out, running over it, and he turns his head slowly and locks eyes with me.

We take our time, exploring and memorizing each other with lingering kisses and touches. We stay there cocooned in the steam until we are both relaxed and needy once again.

This time is slow, a declaration of our love to each other. He holds me tight even after we both reach our release, the tile pressed into my back, my legs wrapped tight around him.

I let him carry me out into the much cooler room after I turn the water off. He sits me on the counter, slipping from my body, wrapping me in a towel.

He rubs it over my skin while beads of water run down his. I'm dry before I know it and I pull the towel from his hands, returning the favor as I slide off the counter.

When we're dry, he leads me back to the bed and we climb in, pulling the covers over us. His arms come around me, and I snuggle against his chest.

"So, tell me. Talk to me until I fall asleep. Keep the angel at bay." I watch as he frowns at the words but nods in agreement.

He talks and talks, telling me about what happens to humans after death. I let the sound of his voice lull me until finally, sweet sleep pulls me under.

I dream of Heaven, of what it once was and what it could

141

be. I see it through Raphael's eyes and I see it through my own. I begin to understand the true purpose of the prophecy, of our purpose.

The light wakes me, not the first rays of morning but the afternoon light, and I realize I'm alone. Arkyn has slipped from our bed some time ago by the feel of the coolness of the sheets.

Clothes are lying at the foot of the bed. Reaching down, I run my fingers over the sweater the color of cotton candy. Not a color I would normally pick for myself, but it's buttery soft.

Beside it is a set of matching lace underwear. Scooting down the bed, I let the covers fall away as I first pull the bra on then the panties. The sweater goes next, and I love the feel of it against my skin. Grabbing the jeans, I slip them on and button them, standing as I do and walking to the door. The sweater is longer in back but shows off my curves. Fluffing my hair with one hand as I turn the door knob with the other, I step out into the hall. I glance left and then right, trying to remember the way we came last night.

Finally, I just start down the hall, hoping there is no dead end. It takes longer than I would have thought to reach the main space again. There everyone has gathered.

Lillian is in the kitchen, and Charlie is sitting at a large island counter watching her cook. The men are sitting on the couch talking low, and that is where I go. Leaning over the back, I wrap my arms around Arkyn.

"You should have woken me." I kiss him lightly to take the sting out of my tone.

"You needed rest." He tilts his head and smiles at me. "You had a very hard week."

"My power healed me," I grumble, spoiling for a fight.

"Maybe physically but not mentally," Zeph states from the other side of the sectional, and I raise my gaze to look at him.

"If you want to fight, I can certainly do that, DYEH-voosh-kah."

"What did you call me?" I straighten and glare at him.

"I called you girl. You act like one, a spoiled little girl." He frowns at Arkyn, who moves at his words.

"I'm no girl, you dick." The room has grown still and silent during our exchange.

He shrugs as if I am of little consequence. Rage floods my system, and I feel my wings and my power start to leak from me.

"You would kill us? Kill me?" His words penetrate the dark haze that clouds my vision.

Fuck.

That's my last thought before I feel the needle in my neck and my eyes widen as I look down at Arkyn's determined face.

I am death.

CHAPTER 28

ARKYN

I'm losing her.

This power is eating her from the inside out, taking her over. Soon there will be no Citlali—just Death.

I look at the other women and for a moment, I hate them. Charlie sees it in my eyes and steps back. Dagen frowns, his brow plunging down over his dark eyes.

'Not their fault, and you know that.'

My head whips around, and I stare down at her. Even so far under, she is reaching out to me.

'They're stronger than I am, can control the power that was unlocked. He...it is too seductive.'

Her words tell me so much, much more than she thinks. I look over at Zeph, jerking my head before spinning and stalking out of the room. I know the others will keep watch over her.

"She spoke to you." His face turns my way as we make our way down the long hallway.

I nod once and he says no more. Finally, we reach the common area. I focus on keeping my mental link with her blocked; I don't want her to pick up on any more of my feelings or thoughts until I'm sure.

"She describes the power as he or it...as something other than herself." I watch as he considers the implications.

"So, she doesn't understand it is she that drives her actions."

I nod and he turns away. "It will be hard for her to admit that the desire comes from within herself."

It will kill her. If she can even do it.

"I think she needs to be taken to Hell." Zeph turns back to face me, surprise clouds his eyes. "If she kills demons," I stop and shrug, "maybe no one else will care but she will. She's a doctor, Arkyn; her whole life is about saving people. It is that part of her that is driving these desires. That and the rage of what was done to her, and I would guess you." I don't like the look on his face, part pity, part something close to responsibility. "She must learn discipline and control."

I shove down the feelings of regret and worthlessness that threaten to overwhelm me. I hate not being able to help her.

"Will you teach her?" His surprise is almost comical. "You have controlled your powers, your rage to the point people forget what you were...what you are. I haven't forgotten. You, more than any of us, can understand the desire to destroy and the regret of it."

Zeph paces away, his muscles tense under his pale blue shirt. I wonder if he realizes it matches his eyes. I wonder why I do.

"I…" He stops and paces some more before finally stopping and looking at me hard. "I'd be honored but…" His eyes turn to the windows again and like before with Lali, I can see his face in the glass. Need. Longing. Both are reflected back at me.

"I will look for her. Every minute you are away with Lali, I will search every inch of this city for the woman." I cross to him and lay my hand on his shoulder. "I understand what I'm asking of you. If I could send her to Heaven with Caliel, I would but I'm scared."

"No, you're right. Hell is better for this. She wouldn't survive killing an angel. It would destroy her. You would lose her to death. We would lose her."

And the war. He doesn't say it, but it's exactly what he means. We don't talk about the number of demons killed daily by the Fallen. The women don't know that there is an entire horde of demons fighting the fucking angels day and night while we try to fulfill this Godforsaken prophecy.

Hundreds slaughtered every damn day and night. Lucifer spends so much of his time creating more. And it's getting worse. Charlie's fuck up in Heaven has caused more and more angels to fall, angels from every tier.

They are falling filled with hunger for everything that's been denied them since the moment of their creation. I can't blame them, none of us can, not these newly fallen. But they have no idea what they've gotten mixed up in.

They want to experience love and lust. Hell, they want to taste life. Who are we to deny them that, but unfortunately, they have chosen the wrong side.

If they would just come to Luc, he would help them. Fuck, any of us would, but instead, they are going to Seraphina. They have forgotten the day this all started. They are choosing to forget the blood that ran in Heaven. My anger flares, and lightning lights up the sky.

They are choosing to ignore what was done to us.

That one simple fact snuffs out most of the sympathy I feel for them. I don't agree with what God has done to them but I can't forget the things done to my brothers on that day and now things being done to these women, who have no choice in the matter.

I don't believe for one moment that their powers only

manifest because of their choice. I think it has more to do with just meeting us and I hate it for them. I look at Zeph. I wonder if he thinks the same thing.

"Zeph…" I sigh, and it's my turn to stare out at the city while he waits for me to finish. "Have you noticed?" I stop again. I don't want to voice my worries.

"Each one is getting worse." He locks his icy eyes on me.

While I appreciate that I'm not the only one thinking it, the very thought is both terrifying and heartbreaking. His face turns back to the glass. "She's out there."

"I think it starts before they choose." There, it's out, and either I'm right or wrong. "Citlali connected with me before she had ever even spoken to me. I think just being in proximity starts the process."

The muscle just under his eye twitches as his jaw grinds.

"Maybe I'm wrong. Lillian and Charlie were in the thick of it quickly, and maybe their hearts chose before their brains did, so I don't know, but Lali fought the idea of being a part of this war. Sure, her wings came after, but something was happening before."

"Your mystery woman has been around the Fallen and Citlali for the entire week."

I have been thinking the same thing. My power has been flowing in and around this city, and Lali's power has been surging since Avalon disappeared. "What if it is similar to radiation?"

Genetics or magic. I'm not sure it matters which is causing it; I only know that if each woman is more powerful and more out of control, it is becoming more deadly for all of us but especially for the women.

"I will find her. I will protect her for you. I promise." I mean the words, and he nods. "I think we need to move her while she is still sedated." He nods again, and we both turn from the city and start back to my room.

As soon as we walk in, I turn and glance at Lillian. "Can you call Luc?" She nods, pulling out her phone. "We are going to move her to Hell. Zeph is going to take her."

"Hell," Charlie whispers. "Why?"

"She must learn control." Zeph sounds stern, unwilling to argue.

"If she doesn't learn to control the power, she will end up killing someone, and that would kill her." I give them an answer to soften Zeph's.

We both leave out our thoughts on what is happening. No need to scare the shit out of everyone. Looking down at Lali, I consider her power, the magnitude of it, and imagine the next woman's power being exponentially greater. Deadlier.

That last is what is truly worrisome. Lali can kill so easily, and while it is a wonderful asset to this war, I can only wonder what using it will do to her.

Luc appears, and we quickly explain what we want to do. He agrees to take her to Hell and lock her in the room he used to train us. He doesn't say it out loud, but I can tell he agrees that she can't be trusted around a city filled with people. Or a world for that matter. Everyone in this room has killed. Everyone has scars from it. I don't want that for her.

A soul so crisscrossed with wounds that nothing will heal, not even her own magic.

CHAPTER 29

CITLALI

*S*creams echo around me.

My heart pounds in terror as I force my eyes open and glance around. Black walls made of some kind of stone surround me, but I can see no door. No exit. No way out.

Why? Why would he do this?

"Hello?" My whisper sounds so loud.

Nobody answers, and I can't see anyone in the darkness.

"Hello?" I say it more forcefully, dragging out the syllables. My anger ignites. "Arkyn." One biting word, the room turns a little darker as my eyes change to the black ones of death.

"That is why he did this to you. Why you are now locked in this room in Hell. Alone."

I know that voice; it's not Lucifer, it's Zeph. The quiet one, the dangerous one. Growing up in Rio, you learn real quick how to spot dangerous people, especially men. Zeph might be the most dangerous I've ever met. That's including Lucifer, the literal King of Hell.

"What do you mean?" I know the answer but I want to hear him say it.

"You have no control, and he couldn't take the chance of you killing someone."

More anger. It makes no sense to me, this rage. I understand Arkyn and the others wanting to protect themselves from me, from Death, but still the rage boils.

"Are you going to kill me?"

God help me, but I feel the power slipping from my body, seeking him, seeking to punish.

"Will you let it kill me?"

"I don't want to but you're right, I can't control it. It's looking for you right now." I want to cry in frustration.

"What is it?" What the hell does that mean?

"It is the Angel of Death." I can't hide the tone, hell I don't even try to. They have all seen it, him...her?

"It is you."

Nope. No. No fucking way. "You are wrong. Liar!" I scream, and it is deafening. Power flies from me as my wings shoot from my back.

I flap them slowly, rising into the air. I don't question how I know what to do. I let them and the power carry me high into the air, searching, but I am alone. Had he ever been here?

"Come back, coward," I whisper. Daring him, begging him.

I rage when I realize magic holds not only me but also the power within this room.

Minutes or hours later, I float down to the ground and tuck the wings away.

Calling out, I smile, hoping all of Hell hears my words and knows his secret.

"All the blood that stains your hands, you above all others deserve death. Death sees all your sins."

* * *

I LOOK OVER AT ZEPH. His face shows no reaction to Citlali's words, but I can feel the tension radiating off him.

"She's wrong, Zeph."

"No, Luc, she isn't. Blood does stain my hands. Angels and demons alike, there's even human blood staining them." He doesn't say it, but I can hear that he believes the words that rang out.

He believes he deserves death. If he does, then so do we all, and I tell him that.

Chana giggles up at me while her hand reaches for him. He smiles sadly as he lets her wrap her fingers around one of his.

Eyes entirely too alert and wise lock on his face, and I feel it then.

A tiny surge of magic.

CHAPTER 30

ARKYN

I can feel her tapping at my brain. She alternates between understanding and a rage that rivals any I've ever felt.

The barriers seem to shake under her assault at times, like now, and I shake my head, trying to push her out. I need to focus on the task at hand and trust in Zeph.

Luc appears right at my side, and even now, after it happening for thousands of years, I still flinch. My muscles tighten and adrenaline floods my system as it readies for a fight. One that I would lose in a heartbeat.

"For fuck's sake, will you stop doing that," I grumble as he grins at my reaction.

"I would say sorry but it is one of my true joys in life." He shrugs, turning his face out toward the city. "You need to find her quickly."

I wasn't expecting him to say that. I feel a sense of dread shiver through me.

"What's wrong?" Now.

Turning back to face me, he locks his celestial eyes on mine. "She has already locked onto his secret shame." Lali.

"She will use it to try to win this fight with him and whether she wins or not, the damage will be done. This woman who already knows of us, I hope she can help repair the damage. He won't give up on your woman, even if it means losing himself."

I don't know what to say; am I sacrificing my brother for my destiny?

"Do you think my Father had His hand in this prophecy?" I nod at his question. "I didn't want to believe it but now I'm not so sure. If He did, you can trust that EVERYTHING has a purpose. He is breaking each of you for a reason."

I glance away, giving myself time to get the nerve to ask the question that I know will not be well received.

"Does that include you?"

His eyes narrow, and he disappears. So, yes then.

Letting my head fall back, I stare up into the night sky. No one knows where God has gone, why He abandoned us, left us to this war. I still find myself searching the skies for Him. I've often sat in the desert or high on mountain tops and looked for the One that made me.

It has often been in anger, my screams filling the silence of the remote places. My power lighting up the skies, calling attention to me, hoping He will finally hear me.

Does He? I don't know but He never answers.

"Do You hear our prayers? Our cries for help? Do You hear our rage? Do You feel it? I don't understand the purpose of this. Why create us this way? Why let us be slaughtered and brought back? He couldn't do it if You didn't allow it." I fall silent and instead listen, ears trained to hear even the slightest whispered answer from the Creator. Nothing.

Wait, what is that? Jerking my head up I look around. It was no whispered word from God; it was fabric against fabric. Someone is near. The hair on my neck rises. Someone is and has been watching me.

I slowly let my eyes drift over all the rooftops near me. There is nothing, no one. That I can see anyway.

"You should come out." I don't yell it, just say it quietly while letting my eyes drift.

My gaze moves farther out, maybe they aren't as close as I thought. The sound of wings drowns out everything else. Shit. Dagen lands next to me.

"What's up?" I look at my brother as he folds his wings away. He takes his time, and I begin to grow impatient. "Dagen."

"Any word on your girl?"

I'm not fooled by the nonchalant tone. "Not really. They've only been gone hours. Learning control can take a while, as you know." He nods at my words. "Why?"

"I just thought Zeph was supposed to be trying to find the next descendant and I couldn't help but notice he didn't come back."

We weren't trying to keep it a secret but the reason for choosing Zeph, I'm not sure if that is information he wants shared with everyone. "Spill it, Arkyn."

"Nothing to tell."

"Didn't your girl just tell us that secrets are what will tear us apart?" His head tilts slightly as he studies my reaction.

I turn away and look out at the rooftops once again. "This is not my secret to tell."

"Zeph?" I nod.

"Do you remember what he was before in Heaven?" Memories of watching Zeph practice his skills play through my head.

"Badass justice-delivering machine." Dagen grins at the memories that drive Zeph to hide his true self.

"Have you seen that part of him here or recently?"

Dagen frowns. "No, I guess I haven't."

"He didn't like his job. He doesn't like the killing. It's why he helps those that he does." Dagen frowns. "The children." I can tell by his total look of confusion he has no idea what I'm talking about. "You really have no idea, do you?"

He shakes his head as his hands wave at me. I don't hurry though; instead I savor my knowing something he doesn't for a moment.

The sound of more wings flapping drags both our eyes to the sky above us. The others have arrived.

"I'm glad you're all here. Arkyn was just about to tell me why Zeph is still in Hell." Dagen smiles as Charlie walks to his side and tucks in against his side.

"Actually, I was just wondering how you could have spent thousands of years around a man and not have any idea what he does when he isn't fighting the Fallen."

Lillian glances between us, shaking her head. "You mean how he works to save children all over the world?"

Dagen's mouth drops open and Charlie laughs. "Really, babe? Zeph runs like three different organizations that work to save kids from every horror you can imagine. Human traffickers, wars, pretty much anything else that can happen to the most vulnerable of humans. I know specifically he has a group of ex-soldiers that do nothing but track and rescue kids being sexually exploited."

"How? How do you all know and I didn't?"

"I asked?" Both women say at the same time.

I chuckle because I know for certain they had to have done more than ask. No way Zeph would have volunteered that information so easily.

"So, the baddest enforcer of all God's laws is now a babysitter." I see the moment he remembers Zeph with Chana in his arms at the desert house. "Oh."

"He's trying to make up for all the deaths." Lillian shakes her head even as she says the words.

"It was his job." Dagen still doesn't seem to get it.

"He has PTSD, if angels or demons can get it." I nod at Charlie's thought.

I actually think it is more like survivor's guilt. He hates his part in Raphael's death. I'm positive that's the driving force behind him agreeing to help me with Citlali.

She is the last link to his best friend. He wants to save her where he couldn't save Raphael. I feel bad for taking advantage of his feelings of responsibility.

"I need to find the woman." I change the subject, and they let me. "Have we traced the call yet?"

"Burner." Shit. I guess it was too much to hope for that she'd use her actual phone.

Dagen pulls out his own phone and plays the recording of the call. Such as it is.

"Tell Arkyn she is at a house with an iron gate on Nieuwe Keizersgracht." That's it. Nothing else, no hints as to who the caller is.

"Helpful," Charlie sighs.

"Well, we know she isn't from here." I lock my eyes on Dagen as he speaks. "No accent. Or at least not one from here."

"I'd say Asia, somewhere." Lillian frowns. "The Fallen haven't settled there in a very long time so I can't really narrow it down much. But I would say not Japan or Thailand, so maybe China. Play it again, Dagen."

She closes her eyes and concentrates as the recording plays. Her head shakes as her finger circles. Dagen plays it again. Head tilted to the side, she leans closer.

"It's weird, I can almost hear a hint of Zeph's accent when he gets mad." Russian. A smile lights her face and she looks at me. "Mongolia, maybe, right along the Russian border."

What in the world would have brought her here? I didn't realize I said it out loud until Charlie speaks.

"Citlali said she felt like the woman was watching her for

the entire time. Maybe the Fallen's magic drew her, or Avalon's. Maybe she has been following the Fallen."

The thought of one of the women being able to track the Fallen is heady. The advantage it could give us.

"Maybe she can sense the other women," Dagen offers. It could be that she could have just felt Lali's pain. "Although it at least seems that she could see through Avalon's shields."

The mention of Avalon has me once again wondering where the ancient place has disappeared to. It would be helpful to be able to hide in plain sight. More helpful to try to learn the magic of those that built it.

I don't know much about those that lived there before. I don't think anyone does.

"Lillian, did you learn anything about those that built Avalon while you were kept there?"

"Not really, only that they were betrayed by someone. Of course, now we know that was Theon. The ancient beings that had lived there when it was an island taught him, and I guess Sitara, lots of their magic or secrets." She shrugs. "There were rooms that I couldn't get into, and some that they couldn't get into."

"Why didn't you tell us that before?" Dagen is staring at her, the look on his face almost comical.

"Sorry, Dagen, in case you've forgotten, this is all new to me, and we have been super busy."

Torryn, who has been silent until now, growls, but Lillian reaches back and grabs his hand.

"How about you change your tone?" Torryn threatens our brother.

"Can we just focus? I'm sorry I even brought it up, it was just a random thought. We need to focus on the woman." I try to steer them back to the matter at hand. "Just before you showed up, I thought I heard something."

They all turn to face out, their eyes scanning over the city.

"She could be watching us right now," Charlie whispers with a grin on her face. "She would have seen us land." She glances over at me, her brows raised.

"I'm positive she was watching the battle the other day, so she would have seen much more than wings." They all look at me.

"Do you think she could be tracking your power?" Lillian's eyes flick up to the sky. "It has been extremely visible."

"I get it. I've been a little out of control."

"A little." Torryn barks out a laugh. The others soon follow, and I grin at them all. "Show a guy that he has almost unlimited power and he goes crazy, lighting up the sky for the world to see."

I feel my cheeks heat.

"You certainly have stumped every meteorologist in the world. The Weather Channel has been running a special report for the last five or six days. Theories of global warming and a superstorm are the most agreed upon." Charlie chuckles.

"Yuck it up, assholes, but depending on how she's tracking me, she could be tracking you too." I wait for that to sink in.

Torryn and Dagen look at each other, and I understand that look. The women they love could be in real danger. A danger that we don't even understand yet. No one wants to think about it, but there is no guarantee that the descendants are all good. There is nothing to say that one couldn't have already chosen the other side.

"We need to find her now." Torryn's eyes narrow on the dark sky.

Agreed but how is the question. Citlali couldn't tell us what she looked like, nothing but that she wore a dark hoodie and always had a book with her.

So we are looking for a possible Mongolian woman with dark clothes and a love of reading. No problem. This should be a piece of cake. I move to the far side of the roof, and my brothers follow. We stand close together and quietly discuss how to find the woman.

We are so wrapped up in our plotting we miss the look of determination on Lillian and Charlie's faces. They wave as they fall over the side of the building, wings snapping open and gliding away into the night.

"Goddamn it, Charlie," Dagen bellows, but Torryn just shakes his head.

"She's got an idea. Let them go. They can take care of themselves." He stresses the can, reminding us that the women are in reality most likely more powerful than us, although it is a bitter pill to swallow.

"I don't like it." It's kinda sweet how petulant Dagen sounds.

"We don't have to. We asked them to join this war and now that they have, we can't treat them like they can't fight in it."

Dagen paces away, staring out at the sky, trying to get a bead on his woman, but they have completely disappeared. My phone vibrates. I look at my brothers, who are focused completely on the city. Pulling the phone out, I glance at the screen quickly. A text from Lillian.

'Celine is gone. We're where we found Lali.'

I stumble over the fact that Celine is gone. What the fuck is going on? Shit, it's because she's in Hell, locked in the cell, and her powers are locked away with her. Now Celine will be looking for payback. She will be even more vicious in her attack.

My spine hurts just thinking about it. Shit. Fuck. This just gets worse and worse.

"I'm going to go look for her. Maybe you guys can see if

you can find a name, a hotel reservation, anything." Dagen's eyes narrow in suspicion, but Torryn just nods.

"Come on, brother, let's go. We can stop at a bar or two as we check the hotels." He winks as he moves by me. The man knows his woman.

I could fly but instead I just jump from the rooftop and land in a crouch before straightening. I get a stupid pleasure from it. Reminds me of the vampires in Underworld, and I happen to love all the movies.

I'm just missing the long coat. The thought makes me chuckle as I start down the cobbled street. I head west along the canal before crossing over one of the many bridges. In no time, I'm at the house standing beside the iron fence. It's empty, the yard and the house. There's not a single sound coming from the property. I hear the same sound I heard on the rooftop and turn slowly. I see Charlie standing down the street, leaned against a wall. Lillian is bold, standing beneath a street lamp, her pale hair practically glowing.

Following their lead, I lean back resting against the fence. Waiting.

If she's out here, we just sent her an invitation to join us. Nothing. No movement. No sounds.

My phone rings, and the sound is loud. Both women whip their head my way. I shrug as I answer it.

"I have a forwarded call for you, sir." I don't recognize the voice, but the number is Demon Bayou.

"Go ahead."

"Where is the other woman?" I glance at the others. They both have straightened and are watching me closely.

"I sent her away to keep her safe. To keep everyone safe." I tell her the truth. "Her powers are new to her. She needs to learn to control them so they don't control her."

"And the other men?" I look around again but still don't see her.

"They are looking for you. My turn to ask a question. How did you find her and us?"

"I have been training my whole life for this." The phone goes dead.

Her whole life. What the hell? Letting my hand fall away from my face, I look around and see movement racing away in the distance.

I jerk my head, and the women rise into the air.

"She's ready for you. Be careful."

Charlie is already focusing on the song. I can tell by the tilt of her head. Lillian manifests the sword and keeping it close to her side in the night sky.

They remind me of the Valkyries of legend.

I look up at the stars in the sky and whisper one last prayer.

"Do not take his hope from him. Even You're not that vengeful."

CHAPTER 31

CITLALI

The power is winning. I'm slowly disappearing. Death will soon be all that is left.

"Are you ready to fight?" His words come from the darkness again.

"It isn't a fight I can win."

"So you're giving up? I didn't think He would send Arkyn one so weak." A light flares, and his face is illuminated and shadowed all at the same time.

His words make me angry, but beneath that anger is sadness. Am I weak? I had never thought of myself in that way. I was top of my class in school. I'm the best surgeon in my city, maybe the country. That is not weak.

"I'm not weak."

"Then you don't think Arkyn is worth the fight." The corner of his lips pull down as he considers me.

"He is worth everything." The words are growled out from between my clenched teeth. How dare he talk about Arkyn that way?

"What if I told you the power, your power, isn't a thing? It isn't an it or him or her?" Now it is my turn to frown at his statement. "The power is you. Death is part of you. Just as much as the other side of the power, the life side."

I feel my head shake. No. No. No.

"You're wrong." He must be.

"I've heard of doctors that think they are gods. Why do they think that?"

My head shakes again as I look down at my hands. I hear the speech from my first day of residency play over in my mind. The doctor spoke of how we hold the power of life and death in our hands. How we choose who lives and dies.

My heart pounds, and I feel my breath struggling in my lungs. The rational side of my brain tells me I'm free falling into a full blown panic attack. I look up at him standing there waiting.

"Help." It comes out as a struggled whisper.

He doesn't move. "I can't help you, accept what you know is true."

I feel his power as it slides over me and slips into my mind. He allows me to know he is there. I feel soothed, and my breathing slows. Sweat covers my body from my panic, and I shiver as I fall to my knees.

"Call for me when you are ready to learn to control the darker side of you, and I will hear you." He disappears just as the tears begin to fill my eyes.

"I am a good person." I whisper it over and over to myself as the tears begin to flow down my cheeks and turn the floor an even darker black.

I watch them drip and splash on the stone for what seems like hours. The five words repeat in my head long after my throat grows hoarse.

Memory after memory plays through my mind. First, it was the people I saved as I tried to convince myself he was and is wrong. At some point, though, the other memories began to escape from where I keep them locked.

The ones that no one knows about, not even Sitara. The men and women who didn't deserve to live. The predators and killers. Traffickers and abusers. Those I judged and found guilty when no one else would. How many had come into my operating room and never left? Ten, twenty, or more?

They died so others could live and be safe.

It was so easy. People die during surgery every day. No one suspected.

The acceptance hits me like a freight train... I have always been the Angel of Death.

I sit silent for a long time; how long, I'm not sure. Time in Hell is different. It could have been days or minutes. I guess that is part of the punishment for those that find themselves here. Eternity has no end, so there is no need to worry about something as short as a day.

But above, Arkyn is fighting. Celine is dying. That thought makes me smile, and I feel that dark side of me smiling out at me.

"Zeph." I don't scream; I just whisper it. I make it a plea.

He appears sitting within arm's length, well within range of my dark power.

"It is neither dark nor light. It just is."

I frown; I hadn't spoken out loud. "What is your power?"

"I have a few, but the most powerful is mind control and reading. It came in very useful in my previous job."

"Which was what exactly?" I don't think I'm going to like his reply.

"I was the Bringer of Justice. An executioner." I hear such sadness in his voice.

It brings the other side of my power to life. Tendrils reach for him, wanting to heal what is broken. He shakes his head.

"No, Lali. Leave me my scars." He blocks my power by reaching inside me with his.

That connection of the two opens him to me slightly, and I see him. Like I've seen Arkyn. I see the wounds that he hides that fester within him. Like Arkyn, he doesn't believe he is worthy. He doesn't search for redemption. There will be no return to Heaven for him, even if the war is won.

He knows there is no place there for him.

This is his home. Here in Hell.

So he thinks, but I know different. Maybe not Heaven but not eternal punishment. I think there's been enough of that.

I close my eyes and reach for Arkyn.

'Find her.' I use Zeph's own power to boost that message and hope it breaks through to the man he cares so much about. It almost breaks my heart how much he loves Arkyn, the baby brother who died trying to save Zeph's best friend. I hear the echo of his promise the moment he found Arkyn dead—I will always protect you. He has been since the moment they awoke here, changed but so much the same.

Lucifer appears, and I know instantly something is wrong.

"Sitara."

My stomach drops at her name, and I shoot to my feet.

"Theon is attacking the temple." He is entirely too calm.

"I must go help her."

They look at each other, and Zeph shrugs.

"She would have to control it or she would kill her."

Lucifer doesn't like that answer but he nods. "You are going with her. The power has been locked down here, but there, it will be as strong as it was on the street." He stares hard at Zeph. "Your job is to keep everyone safe."

"Don't put that on him." I step up to the King of Hell and glare at him, feeling protective of the man that has watched out for Arkyn for thousands of years.

Lucifer grins. "I'm putting it on you, girl. Don't hurt him

or make him have to hurt you." His eyes say he's looked deep within Zeph and knows his secrets also.

"Fuck you," I murmur.

"You aren't the first to have thought that but you might be the first to say it to my face." His face flashes to that of Satan, the one meant to scare all humans and demons alike. I shiver but don't step back. "Good, you are going to need that strength. Avalon has chosen the temple and will only let Sitara in. It is the only reason I came here. I am hoping her love for you will make it consider you worthy, or at least safe."

My jaw drops. He wants me to go back to the place that held me as I lay dying.

Yep. Fuck you.

CHAPTER 32

ARKYN

'*Find her.*'

I startle, looking around. She shouldn't be able to reach me from that cell.

She sounds desperate and sad. I blink, once, twice, and a third time as I try to figure out what to do.

'*Lali?*' Nothing. No response and I don't feel her. She's gone. Looking down at my phone gripped tightly in my hand, I try to figure out who to call. Normally, I'd call Zeph. Second would be Evander, but he's out of commission too. Shit. Dagen? I shake my head.

Instead I pull up the text and hit the call button.

"We haven't found her, but I think we're close." Lillian sounds excited.

"That's not why I called. Lali connected with me." I can hear her landing, stumbling a little. She must have been flying right over the rooftops.

"Is she out?" Both fear and worry cloud her voice.

"I was hoping you might know. Have you heard anything from Luc?"

"No. I'll call you right back." She's the only one I know he picks up for every time she calls. Of course, now we know it's because of Grace.

My phone vibrates, and I answer. "Anything?"

"He didn't answer." Shit. "Something is wrong. Meet us back at the apartment." She hangs up without saying anything else. That more than anything tells me how worried she is; Lillian is polite to a fault.

My wings carry me up and quickly across the city. Owning the building and living on the top floor has its advantages; Dagen is waiting by the opened roof access door.

"They are already heading down." Damn, they're fast. "I think they were just a few blocks away."

I pause on the steps at his statement. Interesting.

"She was looking for us." He nods at my words. How is she tracking us? "Any word from Luc yet?" This time, he shakes his head. "Something is very wrong." He squeezes by me and takes the stairs two at a time. I follow after him, trying to shake the unease from my mind. But it's stuck like glue.

When I step through the door, Luc appears, and his face says it all.

"I just took Citlali and Zeph to Rio. Sitara is being attacked by Theon at the temple. I couldn't help her because Avalon has chosen the temple as its new home. It won't allow me in and it is even blocking Caliel." His face shifts, he is angry.

"I took Citlali, hoping it will recognize how Sitara feels about her and let her in. I don't know who else got in with Theon." His power flutters across us.

Glancing around, I see the others notice it as well. I've never seen him lose control. Dagen's head shakes a minute amount, worry creasing his brow.

"Luc, take us there. Even if we can't get in, we can keep any other Fallen from starting trouble from the outside."

Charlie touches his forearm to make sure he's paying attention. He turns eerie eyes on her before shaking his head, clearing them.

What the fuck is going on?

"Yeah, okay." He sounds completely out of it.

"I think I should stay here and try to find the woman." His head turns slowly my way at my words. "Lali contacted me from Hell." I emphasize the last. "She told me I needed to find the woman."

He nods once, and then they all disappear.

I stand staring at where they were.

No time to waste but I don't have a clue how to find this woman. I can't hear her song, don't have any idea what she looks like. She was close. The thought gives me an idea.

I think we were right that she can track us somehow. I head back out the way I came in, back up to the roof. I think of Lali and my brothers, I think of those that have been slaughtered by the Fallen. My anger, my rage, spikes and my power flows out of me.

Another freak storm covers the Amsterdam skyline. Lightning flashes, illuminating the city.

"Come find me."

.

CHAPTER 33

CITLALI

Z eph is at my side. He is the thing keeping the darkness in check. His words, his pain, his memories, and the knowledge that they could be mine soon or at least ones that look just like them.

The sounds of battle crash through the barrier Avalon has set around the temple. Theon and Sitara are at war.

She will not win. I look over at the man at my side, and his face is set, grim lines creasing the eternal youth of it. He seems to have aged a thousand years in the moment we have stood here.

"She has watched, not fought. She will not win," I murmur what I had thought only seconds before.

He had agreed to stay out of my mind unless I asked for his help.

"She is stronger than you think."

"I have felt his strength in my bones." My voice drops an octave in my anger.

He turns his head and pins me with his gaze. "Then do something to aid her." Easier said than done. "You have yet to try." I narrow my eyes at the invasion. "Cross the barrier."

My heart pounds just at the thought. He doesn't understand the pain and the terror not only of Theon but also the place itself. Avalon held me prisoner, hid me as I lay dying. It did nothing to help me.

"Maybe. Maybe not."

"Get out of my head, Zeph. You promised."

He shrugs, unrepentant. "How do we know it did nothing? Maybe it was why the other woman could see you."

I feel my mouth drop open. I want to argue but can't. I look at the temple. I'm able to see the shadow of Avalon over it. The Avalon from before, what it once was. I step up to the barrier.

"Help me, help her," I whisper at it and I realize that maybe it is sentient. Maybe it had been waiting for Sitara all these years, waiting to help her fight. Theon had stolen and enslaved it, hidden it from Sitara. "I will kill him for what he has done to you," I pledge in a quiet declaration and I let it feel my power.

It visibly shivers, and then we both know. I glance back at Zeph, and his eyes are wide as he stares at it. I know he finally sees it for what it truly is.

The ward wavers just enough to let us in before snapping closed once again. I feel Theon's rage and power punishing it as I stride down the long dark hall I've walked a thousand times. This time, I don't come to heal or learn; this time, I'm here to liberate and destroy.

"Theon!" I scream his name, and silence falls around us as I step into the light.

Sitara's hand comes to her chest as she sees me. I look to my right, and Zeph is grinning at Theon and Celine. If there were others, they fled as soon as they felt my power flare out. My friend nods at me.

"Now is the time to embrace your dark side, Lali. I will be here with Sitara to bring you back to the light."

I can see the dark swirls of mist circle out from me. Cloaking me. Tendrils of death are reaching for those that dare hurt Sitara. That hurt Arkyn. That hurt Zeph. I want to rip Celine apart but focus on Theon; he is the true threat right now.

We haven't seen all of his power yet. Sitara is bleeding from her ears and eyes, and I can tell she would have fallen in moments.

"You dare hurt her here, in her own temple?" My voice sounds strange to me as I let Death take over. "She who has healed and cared for thousands, hundreds of thousands, through the millennia. You defile this place."

"What does Death care if a place of healing is defiled, if a healer is killed?" He taunts me.

"It is not your place to decide. You were marked thousands of years ago, Theon of Lumeria. Your name has been written, therefore you must be taken." I float closer to him and I see that first flicker of fear.

I don't know written where exactly, but it was written. He has been running from death for a very long time, and it just caught up with him.

I, for one, am very excited about that. I hear a commotion and I look over to find Zeph circling around Celine. I let him have her, for he deserves it. I saw his memories of what she did to his best friend and the young angel he swore to protect since that day. I hope it gives him something he needs. That instead of another dark mark on his soul, it heals some that are already there.

Looking back at Theon, I see a bead of sweat trickle down the side of his face from his temple. I raise a brow and smile at him.

"You should be scared." I let one of the tendrils snake out at him and he jumps back but not before it touches him, tastes him.

He reaches for Sitara. Hurt, she's not fast enough to get away from him, and his hand closes around her arm.

"I'll kill her."

I feel his power spike a little. "Can I ask a question?" He frowns. "What did she do that would make you hate her so much?"

"She left me. She was fine with our death sentence. She chose you humans over her own brother."

"You are a child. Spoiled by our entire family, the entire village." She shakes her head. "You caused our destruction. It was your plans that caused His anger."

She turns sad eyes up at her brother's face, and in them, I can see her love for him still there. After all these years and after everything he has done, she still loves him. I understand why she has stayed hidden, stayed away from the fight. She didn't want to kill him. Couldn't kill him.

I have none of that love. He manifests a knife and looks at her with such hatred it almost takes my breath away, and still she smiles sadly at him and waits for him to kill her.

I won't allow that.

I strike before he can move a single muscle. Out of respect for her, love for her, I make it quick. Still he struggles, fighting me and death.

But you can't beat death for long.

He falls, dragging Sitara down with him. Running across the great room, I roll her gently over, and what I see brings tears to my eyes.

He has stolen her life from her, draining her as I drained him.

Death drains away, and I can finally see her through my own eyes. She smiles up at me, her breath labored in her lungs.

"I have loved you since the moment you were brought to

me, since the moment you were born. You have become everything I knew you would be. My daughter."

I see my own tears drip on her face, which is now lined with wrinkles.

"Mother, please I'm not ready. I can't lose you."

CHAPTER 34

ARKYN

I wait for hours, all the while looking at my phone.
No calls.

No texts.

No woman.

Nothing.

I finally break as night turns to morning. Punching the name on my phone, I start down the stairs as I listen to it ring.

"Did she show?"

"No, Luc, she didn't. What's going on in Brazil? It's been hours. And no one has bothered to call."

"Only Zeph and Citlali got in. It got quiet a few hours ago." He sounds worried.

Satan sounds worried. Lucifer is scared. Wonderful. Great.

"I need to get there."

"I know." He appears right in front of me, causing my muscles to bunch. He smirks, but it fades quickly. "Come on, let's see if Avalon will let you in."

We disappear and are in the jungle in moments, maybe

less. My brothers are standing around the perimeter and each of them straighten when we appear.

Lillian comes over to us at a jog. "We are still locked out." She doesn't seem too upset about not being let in. I don't blame her. "You should see if you can get in." She jerks her head at me.

"Has anyone else tried?" Her head turns toward Dagen, who is leaning against a tree.

He holds up his hands, which are burnt and slightly blackened. Ouch.

"Wonderful." I look over at Luc, and he shakes his head while shrugging. "Okay, fine."

Lali needs me, and I will walk through that barrier. I don't fucking care if I come out the other side like a crispy fried piece of bacon.

Stepping up, I draw a deep breath, letting it out before pushing my hand against the barrier. It slips through, and my body follows. Dagen has straightened when I glance back and wink.

"Thank you, Avalon." If I'm not mistaken, the whole place shivers in response. "Lali."

"Arkyn." I'm overwhelmed by the relief I can hear in her voice; it makes my feet move fast as I race through the tunnel to her. I stumble to a stop as I enter the room I laid recovering in for so long because Sitara is laying on the altar. She is an old woman.

What the hell is going on? Looking around, I see Celine chained in the corner, beaten but not dead. Zeph stands between her and Lali, and the look on his face says she won't live for long.

She waves at me, and I want to kill her myself but I hear a sob and turn back to the woman I love.

"Lali, what happened?"

"Theon." She jerks her hand over, and I see him dead on

the floor. "He drained her of her life force as I killed him. I didn't know."

"Shh. Daughter, it isn't your fault. We have been heading to this day for thousands of years." She smiles at me over Lali's shoulder. "Besides, you have found your destiny, your love."

I lay my hand on Lali's shoulder as I glance back at Zeph. *'Why isn't she healing her?'* I think it as loudly as I can.

He shakes his head.

"Lali?" She doesn't look at me. "Lali?" I say it more forcefully. She turns her head slowly. "Lali, have you tried to heal her?"

"I can't get it to work." She cries harder. "I let death control me for too long. I don't think I have the power anymore."

"The power, both sides, are part of you." Zeph steps a little closer drawing her eyes. "Remember what I told you about God. God has the power of both life and death, Citlali. It is still there; you just need to believe it."

"Do you believe your good side is still there?" She bites back at him.

Wow. His face shuts down, and she cries harder. "I'm so sorry, Zeph. I didn't mean that."

"Lali?" I try to draw her attention as he stalks back to Celine. Honestly, I hope he takes his anger out on the bitch. "Think about the love. Your love. You can do this. You healed blocks and blocks of Amsterdam. The news is still talking about the unusual cases. Some are calling it a miracle. You are the miracle."

I cup her cheek in my hand, rubbing my thumb over the smooth skin. She shakes her head.

"You believed in me when I didn't. When no one did. I believe in you." She steps into me, wrapping her arms around me and hugging me tight. Turning her face up, I kiss her deeply, pouring my faith and love into her. Pulling back, I hold her face in place forcing her to keep looking at me. "You can do this, Lali. Save her. Not just for yourself but for us all."

I feel the shift in her powers before she does. Calming power floats through the room. Unlike the death tendrils, this side of her power wraps you in soft warmth.

It wraps around Sitara, healing her a small amount. Whatever Theon has done will take more than one session from the looks of it. But she will live.

Chains clank from behind us, and I turn, leaving Lali to help the woman that raised her. Zeph is pulling Celine to her feet, determination on his face.

"You can't kill me, Zeph. You never could." She grins while pushing her hair from her face.

"You're right. I'm not going to kill you." I frown at his words. I frown deeper when he unchains her. "Avalon won't let you leave, Celine, so prepare to fight. There will be no one coming to save you this time."

She manifests her blade, and I stiffen as she spins to face me but before she can move, I feel Zeph unleash the full force of his power just as mine also breaks free.

I watch as she raises her blade and slits her own throat just seconds before electricity flows into her, bowing her back and flinging her arms wide.

He had made her cut her own throat. Suicide.

See you in Hell, bitch.

CHAPTER 35

CITLALI

*T*hey saved me. My life. My soul.

Zeph reached my brain, showing me the truth of our duality. Arkyn reached my heart, reminding me that everyone is both good and bad, righteous and evil.

I'm both the Angel of Life and Death.

It is a great responsibility. One I'm not sure I want. Can you return your destiny?

"No, you can't."

Goddamn it, Zeph. "Get out of my head, asshole."

Arkyn glances at his friend while Sitara reaches out and grabs my hand.

"You have to control your temper, Citlali." Her voice is paper thin. "I've been fighting that battle your whole life." She smiles at some memory.

"I bet you have stories." His tone begs her to tell him some.

"Don't you dare," I grumble, hundreds of my escapades playing through my head.

"All I'll say, Arkyn, is her teenage years were something close to a second apocalypse. Honestly, I'd take God's wrath any day over her then." She chuckles, but it turns into a wracking cough.

"Let me try again." I reach for her with my power, but she shakes her head.

"I'm fine." She's not fine.

Far from it. I glance over at Theon's body, wishing I could kill him again. Slower. Painful.

Could I bring him back?

"Lali?" Arkyn's voice drags my eyes back to him; he's frowning. "You are good and light."

Is he reminding me or himself?

"It wouldn't work anyway, Citlali."

I glance at Zeph.

"I wasn't in your mind, didn't need to be. You could kill him every day for eternity, and it wouldn't make you feel any better. I promise."

I feel tears pool in my eyes. I had judged these men, their brokenness, but here they are trying to save me from myself when I'm supposed to be saving them.

"We can save each other, Lali." Arkyn moves into me, pulling me against him and holding me tightly. "You gave me what I needed, and I will do the same for you. Every time you get close to the abyss, I will be there between you and the darkness."

Zeph comes near, his pale hand reaching for my cheek as I look at him over Arkyn's shoulder. "I will show you how to control and balance both."

I feel Arkyn smile against my neck and I smile at Zeph. I can do this with these men and the rest that wait outside.

"Sitara, do you know how we can get Avalon to drop the wards?" I realize it's been a very long time since Arkyn came into the temple. The others are most likely going crazy.

"Long ago, I knew the spell, but Theon has changed it.

Maybe they should ask, like you did." She smiles at the thought.

Lucifer asking for permission. I grin at her, and she grins back.

"Is Avalon alive?" I ask her watching her face very closely. "It seems like it is very aware."

"I didn't think so before, but it's been thousands of years and you're right. It seems something more now, somehow." Her eyes travel around the temple, and I know she can see the original Avalon. "I wish I had stopped him. That day. I should have stopped him and the Fallen that day. Protected those that had protected me."

"Who were they?" Arkyn's words draw her eyes away from the walls.

"Honestly, I don't know. I had heard of them long before we angered the Creator."

"I remember when they appeared on Earth, for it caused quite an uproar in Heaven. Many angels wondered about them and why God had allowed them entrance to His playground." Sitara looks over at Zeph as he murmurs mostly to himself, "No one, not even Evander, or as far as I know, Caliel. Luc didn't either or at least, he didn't say."

"Doesn't that seem weird? The most favored of God didn't know anything about a group of beings moving to this planet." I look at both the men and then down at Sitara.

Zeph and Arkyn look hard at each other before spinning on their heels and marching down the hall. Literally marching.

"Go with them, Lali." Sitara's voice is quiet. "Convince Avalon to let them out and then to let the others in, if they want."

I nod once, turning to follow the men, listening to her talk to Avalon and doing her best to undo the wards.

Arkyn and Zeph walk right out through the wards; they

don't even slow down. Avalon lets them and I follow, trusting it... She will let me back in.

Dagen joins us first, his hands held gently at his side. They are burnt horribly, and my power reaches for him instantly, wrapping him in healing light. His hands start to turn pink, the charred flesh falling free. Then it goes a little deeper, healing some of the wounds festering on his soul.

A soft sigh escapes his open lips as he looks over at Charlie. So much love shines in his eyes and is reflected back at him from hers. It is beautiful.

"See, my love, I told you. You are light," Arkyn whispers from where he's stepped behind me. "You are strong enough for this destiny."

"You are my strength," I whisper back.

CHAPTER 36

ARKYN

*H*er power ebbs away, but I still keep hold of her. Luc watches from a slight distance. Crossing the clearing to him, I stop a few feet away.

"She is alive, but it was close." I say it low, not wanting to draw the others' attention.

"Who?" Good grief, how could the ruler of Hell be such a bad liar.

"Sitara," I clarify, barely keeping myself from rolling my eyes like a teenage girl.

"Good."

I don't miss the subtle relaxing of his shoulders. I'm not wrong; I haven't been wrong about his interest in the woman. I've never seen him interested in any woman.

I will see her safe for that reason, above all else.

"Sitara suggested you all ask Avalon for entrance," Lali says, loud enough for everyone to hear. She looks hard at Dagen. "But please take it slow at the barrier. You should feel it waiver if she will allow you."

"She?" Luc perks up paying very close attention now.

"Avalon," Lali confirms.

"She?"

My girl nods slowly. "We think either she always has been or somehow now is sentient."

"The house?" Torryn stares at the temple.

"Yep," I answer him as Lali turns to look at what was once basically her home.

"I can't explain it; I just felt something there. I think maybe she has been waiting for Sitara to find her." Citlali shrugs. "Waiting to be saved...by us."

She looks around the clearing at all of us gathered here then focuses back on the temple. I wonder what she sees there exactly.

"We can, you know, Avalon. We can save you." She stares at the wards. "You can keep us safe. Even Lillian, who you hurt for so long."

We all see it then, the shimmer, like the being let out a long sigh. Lillian stiffens at the mention of her years of captivity, and Torryn glances at Lali, his eyes hard. A warning.

Lali ignores everything.

"You kept Sitara safe for a very long time before the Fallen came and Theon helped them. He's gone now, and it's time for us to pay them back for your years of servitude." Her voice grows hard on the last.

I look at Lillian and watch as her hand comes to cover her open mouth. We hadn't thought of that. Hadn't thought of how Avalon, if it is sentient, has been held as a slave for thousands of years. Forced to do things by those insane bitches and Sitara's maniacal brother. Looking at the rest of my brothers and Luc, I can see they hadn't thought of it either.

Luc walks forward right up to the barrier and speaks low, barely a whisper that even I have a hard time hearing his words.

"I promise I will do everything in my power to protect you and her." He steps through and keeps walking straight inside.

We all stand watching until Torryn speaks. "She let Caliel in." He looks at Lillian and then at Dagen. "That asshole kept going on and on about how powerful he is, and she let him in."

"Because of Grace." We all look at Lillian as she practically floats forward staring at the temple. "You let him in to try to save her." Tears stream down her cheeks. "Thank you." She steps through next.

"I'm with her," Torryn says blandly as he steps forward, and I can't hold in my laugh. He turns his head and winks as he steps through.

Dagen and Charlie stand looking at the temple with me and Zeph. Lali moves to stand in front of me, reaching up and cupping my cheeks.

"I love you. I'm okay now. I'm going to help Sitara some more, but you need to go find that woman," she whispers against my lips before kissing me deeply.

When she breaks away, she looks at the others. "Keep him safe. I don't know if the woman can track you somehow or if Avalon let her see and hear me. Maybe she sensed Sitara on or in me and thought this was her best chance at freedom. Either way, you all know the Fallen will be looking for revenge, not just for Celine but for the loss of Theon."

"We have been fighting them for a very long time," Dagen reminds her.

"According to Sitara and Luc, this is like nothing that has happened before. This is Revelations."

"Well, I for one hope Jesus doesn't come down here," Dagen grumbles and both women turn and stare at him. "I mean I doubt it will happen. He disappeared with God."

"Jesus." Charlie gapes at him.

"Yes, and knowing what humans do in his name already, can you imagine what would happen if he showed back up now?"

I shake my head at him.

"I didn't mean actual Revelations, like in the Bible, Dagen. I just meant the end of the world as we know it. Everything will be different, if we win this war or if we lose it." She actually rolls her eyes before turning and stepping through the wards. She stops a few feet away and glances back smiling.

"I love you." I grin like a fool when she blows me a kiss. "Call or text me."

"Every few hours, I promise."

"The jet is waiting for us," Zeph calls as he walks away toward the truck that's sitting under the low-hanging vines of one of the tall trees.

"We're coming too." Charlie turns and starts sprinting. "Shotgun."

"Dammit." Dagen sulks as he follows her.

Starting that way, I pause and look back. Lali is at the entrance, leaning against the ancient stones, smiling at me. Her hand comes up and she waves; she has that smile on her face. The one that says she knew I'd look back. Power is a heady thing.

Boy, does that woman have all the power over me.

"Get in, loser. We're going on an adventure," Charlie screams out the window, and I shake my head, turning back toward the truck.

My brothers are all laughing when I climb in the back. It suddenly dawns on me just how much these women are changing us. I can't remember when I last saw Zeph chuckle. Dagen seems different, lighter somehow, less worried, I think. Torryn...well...Torryn is Torryn, but everyone else seems better.

I'm better. Whole. At least, I'm getting there. Frowning, I flash on Evander. We need to get Grace fixed.

"We need to go to Hell."

This is the time to go. Luc is busy, and so is everyone else. We just need to get there, since Luc usually takes us.

"Have you ever gone by yourself?"

Dagen nods. "Haven't you?"

I shake my head.

"Really?"

"Yes, Dagen, really." I shrug. "I've only been back once."

"Once." Dagen leans across the seat looking at me closely. "In over two thousand years, you've only gone back once?"

"How many times have you gone?" His disbelief screams many more than one.

"Hundreds and hundreds." He looks up locking eyes with Zeph in the rearview mirror. "You?"

"Same."

"I mean shit, Arkyn, even Lillian's been more than that." Dagen flops back against the seat.

I look at them both confused. Luc has never asked me to go back. No one has. Why?

"Why haven't I been asked to go back?" Forced back. Needed back.

They didn't trust you. You weren't strong enough, my self-doubt murmurs to me.

"Luc didn't want you to spend time there," Zeph answers.

Charlie turns sideways, looking between each of them. "Good God, you two, you have to explain better than that. Can't you see that he thinks it's his fault?"

"You are too good for Hell, Arkyn. You always have been." Zeph glances back at me. "Luc and I agreed a long time ago."

My mouth drops open as I stare at the side of his face.

"Did you take my place?" The whispered words are loud

in the truck. "Did you do things in my place?" I don't say torture or kill, although I know that's what he would've had to do.

Stains on his soul...for me.

He doesn't answer, but his knuckles turn white as he grips the steering wheel tight.

"Why, Zeph?"

The muscle in his jaw flexes as he stares ahead. He doesn't answer, and I look over at Dagen, who shrugs. Charlie reaches back over her shoulder, and her fingers close over my hand. I didn't even realize it was gripping the back of her seat.

"Why?" I say it louder.

He draws a breath. As he releases it, he makes a slight growling sound. "Because out of all of us that died that day, you were truly and purely good. You had not killed in His name, you had not coveted another's position, nothing. You, Arkyn, were exactly as God intended angels to be. Love. For all His wisdom and knowledge, He didn't understand that the roles He gave us would change the very mesh of our being. Or maybe He did. He sent you right to your tribes, and you flourished. It was bad luck you were even in Heaven that day." He shakes his head at the memory.

"I was called back."

He hits the brakes so hard my head bounces off Charlie's headrest.

"Dammit, Zeph." Dagen is rubbing the back of his head, and I see the glass is cracked where he crashed into it.

"Sorry, man." Zeph turns as he speaks and looks at me. "Who called you back?"

"He did. He asked for a report."

"God asked you to return to Heaven THAT day?" Zeph's face is red with rage.

Instantly, I get it but have no idea why the Father would do that to me.

"Maybe He knew we would need you." Charlie tries to offer a kind explanation.

"Fuuuuuck," Dagen murmurs, looking at me.

God wanted me dead.

CHAPTER 37

CITLALI

$\mathcal{F}$ear and anger slam into my brain. Arkyn. Death raises its head.

'You okay?' Even in our minds, my voice sounds dark.

I can feel him trying to calm himself. *'I'm fine, my love. I just found out something that surprised me.'*

Do I press or let him get away with the lie? Then I feel his resolve, not to hide something from me but to be strong enough that I don't think he needs rescuing. Shit.

'I'm sorry. I was just worried.'

'I love you for that.'

I can feel that love and try to send the same to him.

'Okay, text me later. Or not.'

I can feel his laughter. *'Text or mind meld, I promise. I love you.'*

I love you too.

"He's good for you. Balances you." Sitara smiles up at me from her actual bed where Luc had moved her.

"You knew, didn't you?" She blinks unconvincingly up at me. "You knew I would need him. Is that why you've watched him specifically for so long?"

Her eyes flick to Luc, who is sitting in the corner, a baby held in his arms. He might appear to be not listening but he most assuredly is.

"I've watched them all, not just Arkyn."

Luc's eyes raise and narrow on her. "You were the one outside the desert house."

It's not a question.

She nods. "I was so surprised to see the baby that I got too close." Sitara smiles at the little girl.

He looks back down at the girl. "She calms Grace." I look at the doorway where Lillian and Torryn stand. "Yes, Lillian, I know you told them all. I'm sorry... I shouldn't have put the burden on you."

Lillian crosses to him and kneels at his feet, her fingers curving around the baby's head as she looks at Luc's face.

"It is a burden you shouldn't have to bear alone. You have too many already."

Heavy is the crown. The saying plays through my head, and I glance down at Sitara and she nods. Holy hell. I need to talk to her. Alone. I clear my throat and the others look at me.

"Sitara is tired. Would you guys mind..." I imply the 'get out.'

"Of course." Lillian stands, smiling, then starts back to Torryn who had stayed by the door.

Luc looks at Sitara, studying her for a moment before standing with the baby. "I'll take Chana back to the nurse I hired in New Orleans."

He sees Lillian's shocked expression. "I couldn't leave her in Hell with a demon babysitter. The lady is staying at Demon Bayou headquarters so Evander can keep an eye on her."

"Her the nurse or Chana?" Torryn smirks.

"Both." He disappears.

"It's still hard for me to grasp. Lucifer with a baby." I shake my head and then notice Lillian's hard look.

"You don't know him." She spins away before I can reply, and Torryn shrugs, following her.

I cross and close the door, leaning back against it as I turn back to Sitara.

"I didn't mean anything by it." I sigh.

"She cares a great deal for him. She sees him for what he truly is, not what people and God force him to be." Her voice is filled with disappointment. "If you looked hard, so would you."

"I don't not see his goodness; I just haven't forgotten a lifetime of stories."

"I told you many different stories." She looks hard at me. "Why do you think he is so protective of me?"

The question shocks me but as I think back over the last few weeks, I realize the King of Hell has been very attentive to her. I frown. Yuck. She's my mom.

"Not because of that." She chuckles. Thank God, literally. "I knew him before. Not personally but I remember when he was just Morning Star. When he sat beside the Father and was a beacon of hope and goodness."

Oh, well damn, and here I am silently judging him for everything but the way he has treated me. I'm an asshole. A bitch.

"I will do better. I promise." Her lips curve slightly. What can I say, she knows me. It will be a struggle. "But now you need to tell me about that look we shared. What is it you were thinking?"

"Same as you, daughter. He will be the one to rule it all with all sixteen of you to help him. A king in Heaven and Hell." Well, damn. That is exactly what I thought.

"Do you know for certain?" I have no idea of the real scope of her powers.

"No one spoke to me about it, if that's what you mean. I just feel it, more so now than before."

"Now since you revealed yourself or …?" I watch as she struggles to find the words.

"Now that I'm home. I always thought it but now…" She looks around her. "It just… I don't know."

I look around the temple and then I realize she means home in Avalon.

"How long did you live with them?"

"Hundreds of years." Her eyes fill with tears. "They loved us."

"I'm sorry you lost them and Theon but I'm not sorry I killed him." I can't be, not when he was so intent on killing everyone I loved and me.

"It was time. The Theon I knew died a long time ago. He let the need for revenge destroy every bit of the boy I loved so much. I actually am tired, so you go let me rest." I nod and turn, walking to the door but slowly hating to leave her when she is so sad. "I'll be fine. I promise."

I look back and smile. "I love you. You are my only family."

"That's not true anymore."

I guess she's right but still. "I'll check on you in a little bit and heal you some more."

Nodding, she turns her head away toward the wall, and I don't miss her shoulders shaking. I force my feet to move and let her grieve alone. For now.

Joining the others in the kitchen/living area of the temple, I sit down hard on the chair that I used to sit curled in as I listened to Sitara's stories. My brain is working hard to process everything.

Lillian and Torryn are sitting on the couch. I remember when Sitara brought it here. I was tiny still but I can remember all the village men working hard to convert the rooms to living areas. I don't even want to think about what they might have been originally. The temple was built during the time of sacrifices, and even though Sitara was considered a goddess of healing, much blood was spilt in this temple in her name. Blood to call to her.

Of course, I know now she had been gone watching one of the Princes or the King when the people here called to her for aid. It would have been the wards calling her home, not the blood, but they wouldn't have known that.

From the legends I heard through the years, it took her a very long time to stop the killing. I hate that I brought it back to her home. I refocus on the others. Lillian is sitting stiffly. Damn, I've never been good at having girlfriends or really, friends in general. I have no idea how to fix this.

"Lillian." Her eyes turn my way. "I'm sorry. I was judging him on stories I've heard, not his actions."

I tell the truth, hoping it's enough to at least help. Torryn glances at her before looking back at me and smiling. Maybe there's hope.

"He deserves happiness." Her voice is low. "Maybe the most of all of us."

Nodding, I try to understand her zeal.

"He lost everything, Citlali. Everyone. He was forced to become the most hated creature in human history because he dared to stand up for us." She stares at me hard as her words sink in, and I picture the man.

The angel that has done nothing but be kind to me. The angel that cradles a baby so tenderly in his arms and tries to save those that are important to him from pain while saving a world that hates him, that vilifies him.

I really am a bitch.

"You're right. How we gonna make it happen?" I may be a bitch but I'm also super focused when it comes to a task.

Lillian grins. My first real girlfriend.
He won't know what hit him.

CHAPTER 38

ARKYN

*H*ell is just like I remember, and my room is the same. It's like Luc is some weird empty-nester whose kids are at college.

I should have brought my laundry.

Dagen took Charlie to his room, most likely to have sex. I need to find Grace before Luc figures out we aren't in Amsterdam looking for Zeph's woman, or at least who we think is Zeph's woman. Opening my door, I step out and see Zeph leaned against the wall across from it.

"Are you ready? This isn't going to be easy or pretty. I haven't seen her, but Victor was the last of us that did something similar. It was bad and it didn't last this long." Pushing off the wall, he moves to my side as I turn down the hall.

"Do we know what Luc has tried?"

Shaking his head, Zeph leads the way through a part of Hell I've never been in. It's dark and screams bounce off the walls; it is the epitome of Hell.

I don't like it. At all.

He finally stops in front of something that can only be

called a dungeon door. It's thick and practically screams 'stay out.' The noise coming out of it is truly hellish.

Things are being destroyed on the other side of that door, and Grace is making a sound that is reminiscent of a wounded animal. Breathing deep, I steel my nerves.

"Let me go in by myself."

Zeph raises his brow at my words but doesn't stop me. I turn the knob or rather, I try. Zeph grins and whispers some words, and I hear a click. I don't ask how he knows them, and he doesn't offer but he does stand ready as I once again turn the knob.

"I'm here if you need me."

I know my brother. He always has been, it seems.

"Get out, Demon," she growls the moment I step through and close the door behind me.

Grace faces the wall and doesn't turn to face me. The place is destroyed.

Anger and pain radiate off her, and I remember the feeling. It's like two thousand years haven't passed at all. I might not have gone through a long process but I remember waking and feeling so betrayed.

Betrayed. I look at her, at the tattered wings. Wings. She still has her wings, but like the others, they are black. No, not like the others. Hers are blacker than black, whatever that is.

Her hair is still the purest white, although when she moves, I can see it now has hints of silver in it.

"I SAID LEAVE!" She screams, spinning. Long razor sharp claws curve out from her fingertips, and crimson shines from her once beautiful eyes.

So much hate.

It breaks my heart because it's not for us. Another emotion I understand too well.

"I can't, Grace."

She growls at her name. I understand that too.

"I love Evander too much to leave."

She blinks. I'll take it. Just listen, Grace, please.

I start talking to her about me; I tell her every detail. Things I never want to tell another person. Every failure, every self-doubt, every minute of self-loathing. I tell her about thinking I wasn't good enough. I tell her about every worry I've had since we found out the truth.

I talk to her for hours. Every once in a while, I get a flicker of those angelic eyes I saw in New Orleans for just a minute before it all went to...well, Hell.

I finally fall silent, my throat dry. We sit there staring at one another for a few minutes.

"Thank you for listening, Grace." A quiet growl. "I'm not going to lie and say you will ever be the same again." She fidgets at my honesty. "But Evander deserves for you to fight. Not just for yourself but for him. He's spiraling, Grace. Luc will have to do something soon."

I push up turning to leave.

"Like what?" Her voice is more like her own.

"Like this." I wave my hands out at my sides. "Locked away...or worse." Glancing back, I see a tear slide down her face.

Pulling open the door, I step out and close it behind me. Zeph is still standing there. She starts to rage as soon as the door is shut.

I sigh. Failure. I should be used to it.

"No, not a failure, Arkyn. She hasn't been that calm since she woke. Not for anyone. You reached her. Now let's hope she's willing to fight for him."

"Did you hear everything?" Please say no.

"I didn't listen to your secrets, Arkyn. They are yours and yours alone."

"Nothing you didn't already know, I'm sure." I shrug and try to shake the shame of it all away.

"No one can change how you feel about things, and I wouldn't try but I hope you will some day believe me, us when we say you are a good man." He turns and strides away.

So do I.

CHAPTER 39

CITLALI

*Z*eph texted hours ago.

Arkyn is in Hell, in more ways than one. My heart is breaking as I look at Zeph's words again.

'He is trying to reach Grace by telling her about his own anger and shame.'

My poor broken man. If only my power would heal his soul. I can ease his pain but not heal it, not with the power given to me. I hope my love will do the rest.

He will balance my dark side, and I will keep his demons at bay.

Luc appears and looks at me hard. "Did you know they were going to Hell?"

Shaking my head, I walk over to him and watch as he tenses. I did that. I made him uneasy around me.

"I thought they were going to Amsterdam. I told him to go to Amsterdam."

That gets me a smile from the gorgeous man. "You will quickly find out, demons rarely do what they are told."

Nodding, I glance over at Torryn and lower my voice. "How's Evander? Arkyn is very worried about him."

"We all are." He is still tense.

"Can I talk to you someplace private?"

He nods as he reaches for me. The next thing I know, we are standing under a massive tree with branches hanging low. Moss hangs from them, and I know instantly we must be near their beloved New Orleans.

The people of my city strive to be as sinful as the stories we hear of this one. His hand lays on the bark of the tree, and I understand his love for it. I love my jungle, and this tree is amazing. The moss is breathtaking. It looks a little bit like a movie as fireflies light up the canopy like twinkle lights.

Just beautiful.

"What did you want to talk about?" He finally looks back at me, and his voice forces me to lower my eyes.

Now that we're here, I don't know what to say or how to say it. I look at him through Sitara's words, trying to envision the angel he once was.

Again, I figure the truth will be the best way to proceed. "I judged you by the words of countless others who have never known you, not by your actions. I'm sorry for that. You've been nothing but kind to me, and I was rude, among other things." I swallow. "Arkyn loves you, and that should have been enough. I see how the others feel about you. You are a good man, and I will do everything in my power to make sure you get the life you deserve."

He stares at me like I'm an alien. I have left Satan speechless. I'm way more proud of that than I should be, I'm sure.

"That's it. That's all I wanted to say." I pick at the edge of my shirt as he continues to stare at me. Maybe I broke him. Can you break Lucifer?

He finally clears his throat, and his eyes dart around a little. He suddenly looks like a teenager, young and awkward. It breaks my heart into tiny pieces because I can see him then. Not the angel he was before or the devil he is now.

I see him. The man that he is, so unaccustomed to people loving him that he doesn't know how to respond.

I'm going to change that with Lillian and Charlie. I'm not a hugger by nature but I move before I can change my mind and wrap him in the tightest one I can. Shock rolls off him in waves. Me too, man, me too.

I release him quickly and step back and smile at him.

"Umm, thank you," he murmurs, and his voice is thick with the emotions I now understand he keeps locked away behind a wall the size of the one in China.

Lillian was right—this is going to take a very special person indeed. His hand closes around my arm, and I reach my other hand over and pat it even as we disappear. He drops me in the temple, not materializing himself.

I shake my head but smile at Lillian. She smiles back, and Torryn shakes his head at our scheming.

I turn to go heal Sitara, my head whirling with thoughts. He deserves happiness. I won't let anyone hurt him. Death raises her head at the thought, and for once, we are symbiotic in our thoughts; I will kill anyone that tries.

It will take a special person to love him the way he needs.

CHAPTER 40

ARKYN

e couldn't stay with Grace. I've done what I can for now, and we hope it works or at least helps. Luc wasn't happy that we didn't tell him.

He's in a weird mood. I glance over at Zeph and Dagen. Charlie is out searching. We are going to join her as soon as he is finished, I would say talking to us, but currently he's just staring out the windows.

The others look just as confused as I feel.

"So…" I start then stop, letting the word drag out for way longer than it should.

He finally focuses on our reflections before shaking his head and turning to face us.

"Grace seems a little calmer, so maybe you reached her." He locks eyes with me. "You have given her more time, if nothing else."

I nod but say nothing, not wanting to interrupt him now that he is actually speaking. "I checked on Evander. He is also finally getting himself under control but he is different. Losing her…"

He doesn't need to say more. Dagen and I both can't

imagine losing the women, now that we've tasted what their love is like, and Evander had Grace for a very long time in Heaven and then he had two thousand years of thinking she was gone. Only to lose her again, it is unimaginable.

"But your focus here needs to be the woman that Citlali saw." His voice sounds weird when he says her name. I narrow my eyes on him and reach for her.

'Why is Luc being weird about you?'

Amusement.

'I think I almost broke him, but it's fine. He's fine.'

I think there is more to that story but I look over and realize he's stopped talking and is watching me. Waiting.

"Sorry. Just checking in with Lali."

His face softens. Yep. So much more.

"I was saying we need to figure out how she's finding or was finding us. We need to know if she is one of the descendants or something else." Zeph and Dagen nod as they turn to leave.

I hang back, wanting to talk to him about something else. He looks at me, waiting.

"Did God want me dead?" I can see I've surprised him as he blinks slowly. "I wasn't supposed to be in Heaven that day, but the Father called me back. Did He want me to die? I always went to see Raphael when I was in Heaven. He always wanted to know about the tribes."

Luc shakes his head slowly from side to side. I'm certain it isn't a no; it is just his denial that it could be true.

"I don't know, Arkyn."

"I'm sorry, I shouldn't have asked. I just…" I hate that I've upset him. I mean, what does it matter now?

"No. You deserve to know. I'm sorry I can't give you an answer." He turns back to the window.

Watching him, I try to think of anything to say that might make him feel better. So what if God might have wanted me dead all those lifetimes ago? Does it change today any? No. I am still me. I am better than I was. Stronger. Today I have the honor of fighting alongside the best men I know.

It makes me think, to wonder, but I don't voice those thoughts.

No one is ready for that idea.

"I'm going to go search."

He nods once but doesn't say anything as I leave. Everyone else went to the roof and took to the sky, so I decide to head down to the ground. I walk the streets.

Stopping outside a bar, I watch the television screen from the shadows. The news is playing, and I realize our war is becoming less and less of a secret. The mass killings of the Fallen are being noticed, and my brothers and the other demons Luc has fighting them are also.

Humans aren't stupid or blind. They choose not to see the things that are happening around them, supernatural or not.

Evil comes in many forms.

The hairs on my neck stand up, and I use the windows of the bar to look around the street behind me. Nothing. My eyes keep scanning as I turn and start back down the street. I don't see her, but somebody's watching me. Taking a right, I turn down an alley, letting the darkness swallow me. No need to fuel another news report.

I hear footsteps following.

They are what alerts me to my mistake.

It's too late. I know it when I turn and see Seraphina. She smiles, and I see my death in it.

'I love you.'

I send the thought as she closes on me. I roll my eyes up and take in the clear night sky, the stars...the heavens. His creations, or at least some of them, are so beautiful. Bringing my gaze back to the one drawing near, I shake my head. Rotten from the inside out.

"Are you going to fight, Arkyn?"

I nod.

"Good. I do hope you do better than before." Her tone is so condescending.

I smile and a small laugh escapes. "I do too." She pauses, and I can tell she is surprised by my answer. "Can I ask a question before we do this?" More surprise.

"Umm, okay." Her perfect eyebrows draw down in her confusion.

I understand that confusion. I don't think any of us have ever tried to speak to her other than the normal taunts between enemies.

"Do you think He knew all of this would happen?" She blinks. "I mean, do you think He saw even this moment?" A frown mars her flawless face. "Could every step we've made in this fucking eternal fight be one that He foresaw? Does He know how this…," I wave my hand back and forth between us, "will end?"

She opens her mouth, then closes it, and then repeats the actions.

"So He knows you will die here in a dark alley tonight?" I shrug and nod. "He knew you would die by Celine's hands that day?" This time I nod because of that, I'm almost certain.

I watch as her face transforms in her rage.

"I understand it would mean He knew of your hurt and sense of betrayal, knew what it would drive you to do, and still did nothing to stop it."

She screams, and it rolls over the city like a tidal wave. Thousands of years of anger floods out of her and washes over the humans. It sparks their own anger, and fights break out in every corner of Amsterdam. They start killing each other as we stand facing one another but neither moving.

I feel him before he appears. Luc has come seeking the source of power.

"Seraphina," he growls. "Pull it back."

She shakes her head and her lip curls in disdain.

"Let them kill each other." She spins to leave but pauses and looks back at me. "You are wrong."

No.

I'm not.

She and I both know it.

Now, I just need to figure out who God wants dead this time.

CHAPTER 41

CITLALI

I've done everything that I can. She smiles, and the new wrinkles at the corners of her eyes crinkle.

She has always been timeless, ageless, but now she looks like a grandmother. She is healthy, but Theon stole an untold amount of years. I've always thought she would live forever, even before my mind accepted she wasn't human.

To me, she was eternal.

He has killed her after all.

"I have many years before I leave you," she whispers as she cups my cheek in her smooth palm.

"I don't want you to ever leave me."

"That was never His plan."

I scoff and look away from her disappointed eyes.

"Why do you still love Him? Why aren't you angry?"

Sighing, she begins to rock in the chair that had been carved long before I was ever born. The wood is worn smooth from her hands rubbing along the arms. She held me on her lap so many times, rocking me while wiping away my tears. I wait, silently demanding an answer.

"He isn't perfect but then neither are His creations. We all have things to answer for." She falls silent, and I know her well enough to know I'll not get any more of an answer. No more of an explanation.

What do we have to answer for? He left us to the Fallen, who have been killing for thousands of years. Then there are us, the descendants, that at least I know myself for sure hadn't killed or harmed until these powers we didn't ask for were thrust upon us. I ignore those I didn't save it isn't the same as murder.

I don't have anything to answer for.

She clucks her tongue at me. Did I say that out loud? Her shaking head and total look of disappointment says yes.

"You are no saint, Citlali." I hate how her voice sounds and I feel like a small child again. "Don't let your hurt turn you into someone different than the girl I love. The one Arkyn loves." She's right but I can't let it go. Not yet. "I'll be around for a very long time. I promise. But I'm tired, daughter, and I'm alone."

Her words break my heart. "Momma, you aren't alone."

"I am the last of my people."

"Apparently, we all are."

She shakes her head and lets her eyes go unfocused. I watch her getting lost in her memories. Slowly, I rise to my feet and leave her to her many lifetimes, hating that I've only had one and it was too short.

I don't care if I'm selfish; I will try to save her even from herself.

"Are you alright?"

I shake my head at Lillian's question. "She's giving up. I've done everything I can but I can't return the years he stole from her."

"It must be awful for her. She has lost everyone she ever loved."

I grit my teeth. "She hasn't lost me."

She gives me a look filled with sympathy, but all I see is pity. I don't want it. So I run. Out of the temple and into the jungle. I run until there isn't another human for miles and miles. Until the jungle swallows my screams. A jaguar calls out, responding to my grief.

"I will save her if I can."

I scream again when his voice sounds from directly behind me.

"Goddamn it, Luc." My words are breathless.

"So true."

My lips curve even as I try to fight it, and he returns the smile. He is breathtaking. With that smile on his face, he is The Morning Star. The ultimate temptation. It's strange because he isn't the type of man I'd normally be interested in, but somehow he is everything. Everything appealing even without looking like it.

I blink, and he's watching me, his cheeks slightly pink, and he looks so uncomfortable. I chuckle and shake my head to clear the thoughts away.

"Has Arkyn found her?" I can tell he appreciates the change of subject.

"No, but he did find Seraphina."

My heart stutters. "Is he…"

"I wouldn't have told you like that, Citlali."

Apparently, it's my day for hurting people's feelings. "I'm sorry, I know that. She was just so awful."

"That she is." He looks around when the jaguar calls again. "She just walked away though."

What is going on? I don't know much about her or any of the Fallen, but that doesn't sound right.

"Why?"

"You'd have to ask Arkyn. He said something to her that shook her." His eyes focus on me once again.

I just shake my head. I have no idea. "Did you ask him?"

"No, and he left almost as quickly as she did. He did ask me a strange question before he went out to look. He asked me if God wanted him dead."

I see black at the thought. "Did He?" My voice is gravelly.

"I'll tell you what I told him. I don't know. I hope not because Arkyn was the best of us. It makes no sense."

No, it doesn't.

What's going on?

"Can you take me there after I tell Sitara?"

He nods and takes us to the temple in seconds. Torryn stands when we appear, and so does Lillian.

"Just give me a few minutes." He nods again as I start into Sitara's room.

I can hear him telling them what is happening.

"Go, I will be fine here. Avalon will keep me safe, and you have done all you can."

"Something has changed or is about to." She nods at my words. "Arkyn. I'm worried."

"Your man is very smart and has a kind heart." She pushes up from the chair, then crosses and pulls me down to her. When did she become shorter than me? She hugs me tightly, and I let go of the thought. "Go, fulfill your destiny."

The words are whispered as she releases me and turns her head, smiling at the young looking man in the door.

"I will come and check on you as soon as I can," he promises, and she nods.

The others are waiting, and he takes us all to Amsterdam in seconds, making me wonder why they bother with any other mode of transportation. He disappears as soon as he drops us at the penthouse.

"Where's he going?" I ask anyone who is listening.

"He has lots of responsibilities," Torryn answers, and his tone is hard.

I'm not sure I'll ever be a part of this group. They need me but they don't like it. I rub people the wrong way; it's one of the reasons I went into surgery. Less people-ing. I'm not good at it and normally I don't care but with these people, well, I do for some reason.

"Because you could have a family," Zeph's voice calls through the door even before he gets it open.

"What have I told you?" I grin at him.

"Sorry, little sister, but you think too loud." He crosses to me and pulls me in for a quick hug, surprising me. "Just give them and yourself time, and it will all work out."

"I'm not so sure about that."

Arkyn steps through the door and relief floods my entire body and soul. I squeeze Zeph as I release him and step away. We meet in the middle, and Arkyn's hands cup my face, pulling it to his. He kisses me like he's drowning. When he breaks away, I'm struggling to catch my breath.

"Hi."

"Hi." I smile up into his eyes. "Are you okay?"

He nods as he reaches down and grabs my hand. He turns and starts to pull me down the hall.

"Hey! Are we going to talk about why we were brought here?" Torryn yells.

"Later," Arkyn grumbles, not even slowing.

My stomach flips at his aggressive tone. It only takes seconds for us to get to the room we had been in before. If I had thought he seemed to be drowning before, as soon as the door closes, it is like he's ravenous. Electricity skates over my skin from his barely controlled power. He bites and licks at my skin even as he is pulling my shirt over my head. In less than a minute, I'm standing naked before him panting.

He's upset about something, I can tell, but I'm not complaining. I'll happily let him take it out on me.

CHAPTER 42

ARKYN

She'll let me do whatever I want. I can see it in her eyes, the desire to lose herself in the moment, in us. I need to dominate. To rule her.

Her breaths are labored from uncertainty as she waits for me to make my next move. So I do. I push on her shoulder, and she drops to her knees. She reaches for me, but I step back and she glances at me in confusion. Ignoring that look, I undo my pants and shove them down my legs, stepping out of them and back to her.

"Leave your hands down."

Her cheeks flush at my command. Taking myself in my hand, I guide my dick to her mouth. Her tongue comes out and licks over her lips as she opens to me.

I start slow, with every intention of taking my time, but then she flattens her tongue and rubs it over that sensitive area just below the head. I force myself deep, feeling her throat fight to adjust as I hold still there. I only draw back when I know she needs a breath. The entire time she is licking over me.

My hand comes down and circles loosely around her

throat as I repeat the process, and she moans. I watch as her hand disappears between her legs.

"Let me see." It is a command.

She raises it, and her fingers are glistening with her wetness. All my plans go out the window. Instead I pull her up, letting my cock pop free from her reddened lips, and toss her back on the bed. She laughs as she bounces, and I can't help but smile at her.

This is true happiness. Lust and love all rolled into one. Complete confidence that her laughter is not at me but with me. I crawl over her, and she shifts her legs wide, giving me access to her core while her hands pull my face down for a soul-searing kiss. Pushing into her, I seat myself fully. Her heels push at my ass, wanting more. Our bodies are fused as one as I wait a beat before pulling back. We are both close, our emotions driving us higher than our actions. We both become frantic, our bodies slapping together as I pound in and she shoves her hips up to meet me.

We come together, her cries muffled as she bites at my neck. We both pant as we catch our breath.

"I wanted that to last much longer," I murmur against her jaw as I kiss it before moving to just under her chin on my way to her breast.

"Sometimes, you really just need quick and hard." She grins down at me as I roll my eyes up. My tongue flicks out and over her taut nipple before I suck it into my mouth. I let it go with a quick, hard bite.

"I guess you're right." Rolling off her, I pull her into my side after we untangle our legs.

She looks at me in silence for a few moments and then finally speaks. "So, what happened?"

I sigh, knowing the break from reality is over. "If we are going to talk about it, we should join the others."

Lali nods but burrows closer, and I'm happy I'm not the

only one that would like to hide from life and the war for a few minutes longer.

It ends up being much longer as we fell asleep in each other's arms. I wake slowly, confused by the heat surrounding me, but smile when she shifts slightly and mumbles something incoherent in her sleep. I realize we haven't slept in days, none of us have. Sliding very carefully out from under her, I pull the covers over her body and move to the end of the bed, bending down to grab my pants. After I pull them on, I turn to go find us some food but stop at the door. I turn back and look at her, just watching her sleep.

Thankful.

I run into Dagen in the hall, and we walk to the living area together. The others are there. Lillian is cooking. Charlie is watching the news, and Torryn and Zeph are in a deep conversation in the far corner.

"Sorry, guys, we fell asleep."

"I think we all need to rest." Zeph looks over at me. "We won't win the war if we aren't fit to fight."

Are there really any winners in this war?

CHAPTER 43

CITLALI

I hear their voices as I stretch; they're arguing about something. Ninety percent of me wants to burrow under the covers and ignore it, but the other ten percent pushes me up from the mattress. I see a closet and hope there are some clean clothes that will fit me.

I grin when I see things that will fit me perfectly. Sweet, sweet man. I pull out army green cargo pants and a black tank. Padding down the long hall bare-footed, I try to catch more of the heated conversation but I only get snippets.

Something about the war and not anything about how to win it. Arkyn is very upset. I can feel it. I can hear it. My feet speed up without me asking. I stride into the living area, and everyone stops talking.

"So…" I look right at Arkyn. "Time to talk."

I can tell he's not excited about it or maybe just not about saying it out loud.

"Luc said you told Seraphina something, and whatever it was, it spooked her."

His brothers all turn and look at him, and he straightens. There is the man I knew he could be, looking out at them. I'm proud but also scared of whatever he's about to say.

"I asked her if she thought God knew all of this was going to happen. If He even now knows the outcome."

It's like all the oxygen has been sucked out of the room. I look around and I can see them all trying to form an argument against Arkyn's revelation, but no one can.

"He summoned me to Heaven the day it started. I wouldn't have been there. I think He wanted me dead." He looks hard at his brothers. "Which could mean that He wanted me to be this."

He points at himself.

I draw a breath then let it, and the thoughts running through my head, out. "God made you a demon."

All hell breaks loose. The Princes all start yelling at each other, unable or unwilling to believe that God could have orchestrated this whole thing.

Do I believe it? I certainly don't want to but if He's all knowing, how could He not know what was going to happen that day? Hell, what is happening right at this moment?

Would He do that, set this all into motion, or is He maybe not as all knowing as we were led to believe? I know better than to make that suggestion but I look at Charlie and I can tell she is having at least a few of the same thoughts. I jerk my head. She and Lillian follow me out the front door and up the stairs to the roof.

"What do you think? Not about my statement, I think maybe that was shock." I smile my most awkward smile that makes me look slightly deranged. "More about what Arkyn thinks. Could this all have been orchestrated—them and the war?"

"Us," Lillian says what all three of us are thinking. "Would He have let my family be slaughtered?"

I can hear how heartbroken the thought makes her.

217

Charlie moves to her right side, I go to the left, and we both circle her with our arms.

"This is so fucked up." I nod at Charlie's statement. "Like beyond."

The door creaks a tiny bit as the boys open it. They come through one by one. Zeph is the last and he stands back a little as the others come and form a protective circle around us. They don't do anything but stand there, letting us cry. To lament the injustice of our entire lives.

Slowly, we come apart and turn to our respective loves, each stepping into their open arms. Taking and receiving comfort. After a few moments, I pull away from Arkyn and turn walking to Zeph and wrap my arms around him.

The sounds of surprise let me know that I've once again done something that isn't done. He hugs me back though tightly. The revelations have shaken him.

"So much death." He murmurs it, and I don't think he realizes it.

When I pull back, his eyes are locked on his brothers but focused on Arkyn. He told me the story, and I know he is thinking of that day and Raphael.

"Maybe there was absolutely nothing you could have done."

His face turns back to me and he nods, but I can tell it doesn't bring much comfort. All the things he had done in the name of the Father, and if our thoughts are true… Well, it's too much. We all head back down to the living area, except Zeph. He stays on the rooftop, looking out at the city.

We've come to no conclusion. Made no decision on how to proceed. The consensus is that we continue as we have been, or how they have been.

Find the women. Save the world.

CHAPTER 44

HER

.

They are going through something. Something big. He is alone on the roof. The others have left him after they came together. The one I was shown held him for a few moments while the others looked on, shocked.

I think about calling again but I'm not sure. They are different...more.

The wings were a surprise.

They are what I was taught to hide from and to fear. The others that had been at the house, them I fear. The house showed them to me. A warning.

My phone vibrates, and I look away from the rooftop. It is Aroon. He checks in daily. Answering, I glance back at the roof, and the man is still there. He looks lonely.

I feel lonely. It has been a long hunt.

"Hey." I try to sound happier than I am.

"Little sister, any more interactions?" He is not one to make small talk.

"No. I think they may be trying to find me, but so far, they haven't. The women were searching for me, but I don't think they have any actual way to find me."

"Good. It is not your job to help them, Misaki, or interact with them at all. The brothers sent you to observe only. It is what we do. We watch and we wait."

I want to argue but I know it'll do no good. "I know." I don't mention the phone calls. The repercussions would be dire. "I'll call and update you as soon as I find out anything else."

"Misaki, try to find their base."

I glance at the Demon Bayou Rum office building.

"I will." I feel awful not telling him, but something more is going on than what we've been told. I can feel it in my soul. "Goodbye."

I hang up before he can say anything else and shift a little. The chair is uncomfortable but serviceable, and I've been sitting in it for too many hours watching the building. Standing, I stretch my back and neck before refocusing on the building.

He is looking right at me.

I stare for a minute, wondering if he can see me through the glass this far away. He takes a step toward the edge of the roof, and I spin, running for the door.

Running for my life.

THE END...

until next time.

EPILOGUE

CHOSEN SHADOW COMING SOON

ROLOGUE

I DON'T LIKE the plan but I will do it if it ends this war. If it gives the others their chance at a real life, one not saturated with blood and death.

Lucifer looks at me, saddened by his request.

"There is no need, my lord."

His head shakes at the title, but it is what he became the day he chose us. The day I awoke, changed and angry but still able to recognize the sacrifice, I chose him. I love my brothers, but my loyalty and life belong to the one that made the ultimate sacrifice and still does.

He gave up not only his life as he knew it but also his very identity. He became Lucifer… Satan… the very King of Hell. For us.

"I will leave as soon as I talk to Zeph." I smile a little, thinking of the shadow I've noticed in the darkness. She will be a perfect match for my friend.

"Victor, please know I don't ask lightly. I wish I didn't have to but..."

I transform, leaving him looking after me.

My death is a small price to pay.

ABOUT THE AUTHOR

S Lawrence is an emerging author of paranormal memoirs. She is a mom, a wife, a veteran and a fangirl. She lives just outside New Orleans and can be often found wandering the streets of the Quarter.

To keep up to date on new releases and get in on some awesome giveaways head over to her website at https://www.slawrencewriter.com/

To join her reader group the Myth Mavens go to https://www.facebook.com/groups/1946397745641272/

ACKNOWLEDGMENTS

When I wrote Celtic Fire, I had no idea I would end up here. And I couldn't have, not without the support of so many people. My husband, who I can't even begin to thank for his support and the work he does to make my dreams come true. My kids, for endlessly believing that I am going to be famous and that everyone will love my books.

My best friend, who spent countless hours reading and checking for mistakes. She has always believed more in me than I do myself. She is Louise to my Thelma.

To Summer, for amazing editing and support. I was looking for an editor and I found a friend.

To those readers who took a chance on Celtic and have supported me through that series as I found my voice, I can't thank you enough. There are no words for what you've done for me.

If you just found me I hope you like it.

Susan

Made in the USA
Columbia, SC
04 August 2024

39610916R00126